I0672122

DOMAIN OF THE LOWER AIR

DOMAIN OF THE LOWER AIR

SHORT STORIES BY
MARYANNE KHAN

BRP
Broadkill River Press

Copyright © 2011 Maryanne Khan
All rights reserved.
Printed in the United States of America.

ISBN 978-0-9826030-4-8

BRP
Broadkill River Press

James C.L. Brown, Publisher
Broadkill River Press
104 Federal Street,
Milton, Delaware 19968
E-mail: the_broadkill_press@earthlink.net

DEDICATION

I thank my beloved husband, Raja Khan, for his support and encouragement in my choice to dedicate my life to writing and am grateful for his unwavering faith in me. I thank my lovely daughters, Chiara Del Gigante and Alexandra Del Gigante and son Tanvir Khan, each of whom has become a wonderful young person of whom I am very proud. My thanks also to my friend Joe Amato who is always generous with his time and ever willing to share his considerable experience. My greatest appreciation as a writer is to my former teacher and now mentor of thirty years, Jamie Brown, whose constant support, guidance and wisdom have been invaluable and that have now resulted in *The Domain of the Lower Air.*

Acknowledgements

"Good Friday," *The Broadkill Review*, Vol. 2 No. 6, Milton, Delaware, November 2008.

I Never Lie to You, with artist Caroline Ambrus, Irrepressible Press, Canberra, ACT, 2007.

"Grandma Pharaoh and Me," *Cottonwood*, University of Kansas, 1992; *Four W*: Vol. 5, Charles Sturt University Press, NSW, 1994.

"Casa La Matta," *Four W*: Vol. 18, Charles Sturt University Press, NSW, 2008; *The Broadkill Review*, Vol. 4 No. 6, Milton, Delaware, November 2010.

"Shattered," *Connotations Press*, An Online Artifact, 2010.

"Lacey," *Sulphur River Review*, Austin, Texas, 1994.

"Diving Too Long," *Redoubt*, University of Canberra Press, ACT, 1995.

"Sweet My Infant Born to Die," *The Broadkill Review*, Vol. 1 No. 1, January 2007; *Wet Ink, The Magazine of New Writing*, Issue 10, Wet Ink Magazine Inc., Adelaide, SA, 2008.

DOMAIN OF THE LOWER AIR

"He found you as dead men, such were your transgressions, such were the sinful ways you lived in. That was when you followed the fashion of this world, when you owned a prince whose domain is in the lower air, that spirit whose influence is still at work among the unbelievers . . ."

—Ephesians 2:1

Contents

GOOD FRIDAY

We carried the cross shoulder-high flanked by the tall wax candles in their polished brass holders and Zio Pasquale was head of the procession on account of his name – 'Pasquale' for Easter. That was after father La Favia had said that the Feast of the Resurrection conquered the Friday of Death and therefore took precedence, and that put an end to the dispute. So Zio Crocefisso Baglione had to walk second, behind Zio Pasquale because the Resurrection triumphed over the Crucifixion and so 'Pasquale' came before 'Crocefisso.'

As always, we had sent to the coast for fish, brought out our black clothes, and walked in the procession that started at the church at three in the afternoon—which was the time the veil had been rent in the temple to show the end of hope on earth.

And this was true because Zio Pasquale always said "There is no hope for poor devils like us; we are *poveracci*, and life is only what it is."

And he was right. And even Jesu' was a poor man, just like us. And just like us there was nothing He could do, and they tied His wrists and beat him, and hung Him on the Cross. So on Good Friday we carry Him on our shoulders, like a burden of ours, and He belongs to us and His pain is ours—that day and every day ever after—like the salt-tax and the cholera and the lack of rain for the wheat and the grapes—weighing on us in His misery and His suffering, and the drum beats low and empty in the streets like the heart in the breast of a poor man, hungry and solitary, knowing there is nothing he can do.

And the procession passed the wine-shop in the piazza with the shutters rolled half-down and the pump at the door running the water Cecco Ubaldi uses to cut his wine, and the bread-shop where the scale is never right and the house of the widow of Cesare Cotti, who mourns old Cesare with any man would help her tell the beads, and down over the cobbles past the sign that says *Poste Italiane* and where the heirs of Francesco Tibaldi still cannot withdraw his life-savings from the account because the postmistress denies there ever was one. And on and on through the village past the shops and *botteghe*, the houses and streets standing still for Good Friday.

And Jesu' was a carpenter and Zio Crocefisso Leone is one too but not the same kind as the Povero Jesu' because Zio Leone keeps the wine-flask in his workshop and has a long-handled-scythe for cutting back the weeds and it stands behind the door, and he works the wood with saws, chisels, and sharp knives, but he has a another knife, just as sharp and even sharper, that he carries hidden in his jacket next to his heart, because he has sworn to keep it for the father of Pia Maggiore who refuses to give her to him for his wife.

Father La Favia said that Jesu' was the Son of Man who had died on the Tree. And Silvestro Maggiore said that Zio Leone was a man who cut down the trees on the land of others, and once he had cut them and stolen them away it was the same as having cut out his own heart and that Crocefisso Leone would rot and die, sure as the wood cut from those trees.

But Zio Crocefisso Leone said, "And what can poor devils like us do any different? This is our fate—we are *poveracci*, poor people, and the world is made for those like us."

So this Good Friday, behind Zio Pasquale came Zio Crocefisso, and they and five others carried the cross of heavy walnut-wood with the figure of Jesu' bigger than all of them, bigger than a man and heavier in plaster, with the tears painted coming down from His eyes to behold the iniquity of mankind, the bier draped in purple velvet edged in black with the chanting women on either side, the other black-veiled women of the procession behind, and the men in the Piazza della Chiesa with their jackets over their shoulders and their faces grave under their hats, smoking Tuscan cigars and quiet out of respect. But not walking in the procession because that was a thing of women and a thing of the Mayor.

And it was a thing of the Mayor because Don Silvestro Maggiore was bigger in name and bigger in body than any other man in the village. And everyone said that had he lived in the city, in America, Don Silvestro Maggiore would have been a boxer, a fighter, trained to live by his wits and his fists. But here at Monticelli, where no one fought in a ring for pay, they say he fights all the same, but in his heart.

Before the procession, inside the church, Don Silvestro had said out loud with all the others, "Lord have mercy; Christ have mercy . . ."

He had said, "Lamb of God who taketh away the sins of the world . . . Grant us peace."

But outside on the steps with them all standing round he said. "And let him who has taken what was never his make restoration to the rightful owner—let him return what is stolen to the proper owner," and he spat at the feet of Crocefisso Baglione.

Then old Anna Moretti began to cry out in a loud voice and her sister's niece and the widow of her son (who everyone knew was the son of Don Silvestro), took her away to her front door along the Via Crucis and made her go inside.

"Let the man who is raised like the Bad Thief on the left hand of the Saviour make restoration," Don Silvestro said. "So that his sin may be forgiven him and his soul not burn in hell."

So on Holy Saturday, in the quiet of the evening of the Vigil, while the Saviour was sleeping, while I was walking with my sheep, I saw Zio Crocefisso ride up to the house of Don Silvestro and wave his *fiasco* of wine at the curled white shaving of pale moon above the roof, and heard him fall to cursing the household and the dead of that family before them, shouting *"Alli mortacci tua*, Don Silvestro Maggiore!" and I saw him draw the knife kept in the dark pocket next to his heart and I saw him kiss the blade, and his horse reared up and threw him.

And yet, inside the house, they say they heard nothing.

So on Easter morning they found Don Crocefisso white and dead in the roadway, with his own knife in his heart and his horse, un-tethered, standing mutely by.

But I had seen Zio Crocefisso and Don Silvestro, and the story I knew was different.

And despite all this, and maybe because of this, the sun still rose the same over the mountains to light, without warming, the hearts of poor devils like us.

I NEVER LIE TO YOU

Tomorrow is my birthday, and today I am the same. I shall always be the same, I shall never seek the wished-for, I am never afraid. Tomorrow will change nothing, looked on from today.

Time is no gift, no breath a miracle. I would stay the same should I live the eternal cycle of this one life unchanged. I would always choose what I know. I know everything there is to know. I know nothing. I close the shutters, I veil my eyes, I shade my face from light. I lock my mind in a darkened room and this is a good thing.

I feel no pain. My hands are cold, my arms are cold and this brings me comfort. I want for nothing. Nothing is missing, all is in its place. Nothing disturbs, nothing mis-fits. All this goes explained, all is predictable, nothing is dangerous.

There is nothing I care for more than all else, nothing I'd risk for. I can't close my hand to keep what I have, or open my fingers to let it fly, sand running off my palms, streaming in the wind. I am satisfied only by knowledge of the grand and infinite, there's no solace in small things—the dip of a wing, or words on a page. The world is calculated in numbers and quantities; things beg definition, things are what they seem. I spell out names, compare costs, number off volumes, as long as what I mean is clear. I don't marvel at the wonder of it when something spills into my cup. I take it on the tip of my finger, unthinking, tasting what I have. I have nothing; I am happy. I never need to sleep.

There's nothing I'm entitled to, nothing I want. There is no such thing as a needy soul, the unloved heart, the touch of fingers on a face. My hands aren't beautiful, conveying words. My hands are mute. I trace the line of your brow with a finger but never soothe. There is no frailty in gesture. My heart never bleeds.

I am of water, broad as a lake. My mind is fathomless, holding secrets. I hold no secrets. I am nothing but a mirror to the sky, my shallows lie still. I am a small piece of driftwood in the palm of your hand, gouged and roughened, worn smooth, tumbled. My spirit lies still and asks for nothing. As I give nothing. My mind stays set, thoughts peel in layers in ever-decreasing circles. Cobwebs show activity, ladders stretch nowhere; all footings are safe. All is a circle, closed, hooped in iron, rusted. A bright circle of water at the fall of a stone, then silence. The float of a lilypad, a pink flower with petals of porcelain. The stab of a reed. Each day drops like a leaf with never a ripple, nothing moves, nothing flows. No dip, no surge, no plunge. There are no means to ends and no end can justify the slightest pain. Each instant of being remains undisturbed, unperturbed, and I want for nothing.

I am not becoming wild, I am not dangerous.

I know all the paths to hope and I choose none. I know every way to love, and I choose none. I have cared deeply for my spirit so it blooms like a moonflower—only at night in the slate-grey dark, only in half-light, away from the day. I tell you no lies. Nothing is hidden.

I never name you, never grant your reality. You aren't known to me by your many names, you are never young and green, blue and night-cast, older, wiser, sombre, you are never joy. There's no sound around you, you are nameless. You are colourless and tasteless. I ignore that I forget you—you are unknown.

Are you afraid yet? Have you lost your place?

I'm going out now. I'm going where you are most afraid. I'm leaving you when you are most afraid. I leave you there sleeping, crying out softly in your sleep what you would call out loud awake. I creep from your glass room and turn the handle of the door, laying my palm against it, pulling gently, to muffle the click. You don't know that I've left you and my going won't rouse you. I do this unthinking, easily. I wake at three to see if I can leave you yet again, and I always see I can.

I'm going now, to where you are most afraid. You always wake to find me gone, my best beloved.

I come to the place where you lie asleep. I never speak. Your mind follows the curves and billows of shared thoughts. You hold me in your sleeping mind, and I am a pale flame burning in the sun, invisible to all but sleeping eyes. I cast no shadow, I walk in your mind. You see the sea through me as if through windows, through glass. I may be an echo, I may be the first sound in the world. I lead you to places you remember when you wake; I give infinite knowledge with the lay of my hand. I lead you in breathless expanding visions to recognize me, and therefore yourself, in things that are miraculous. As you sleep, I hold you in my mind.

You wake and I am always there, my best beloved.

GRANDMA, PHARAOH AND ME

"Wanna do something?"

"Not today."

"Whatcher doin' out here?"

"Running away to Egypt," I said. "What's it to you?"

"I'm gunna run away too some day. Where's a good place?"

Luddy couldn't go to Egypt like me because of the coins. There were only enough for me and he knew it, so he was trying to think of somewhere as good as Egypt, only there isn't.

"My Dad says your Ma's going to lose the place," he said.

"You don't know a damn thing Luddy Van Dorn," I said and it was true. "Your Dad neither." They can't hardly speak English let alone know other people's business.

"Got a jar for yabbies," Luddy said, like every Saturday.

"It's my creek and I say who goes fishing for yabbies," I snapped.

Luddy got a shock. He blinked hard, like Mama does, only she does it all the time. She blinks as though she's resting her eyes and looking at what's going on in her mind in case she missed something. With Luddy, though, it was just surprised.

"Wasn't your yabbies last Saturday."

He was scooping up water in his jar and tipping it out slowly, just in case. As if yabbies crawled into jars by accident. Like I said, Luddy is a pretty dumb boy.

But he was right. Last Saturday they were Grandma's yabbies—now I didn't know who they belonged to.

"Buzz off Luddy!" I said. If he didn't go right then he'd see me cry.

But he kept fooling around with his jar. "Mickey Mouse Club's today," he said kind of sly as if I'd forgotten who had the only TV for miles around. But right then I didn't care about the stupid TV, or the Club or anything. He was still hanging round. I poked at a stuck branch in the creek.

"What do you think it feels like to be dead?" I asked.

I thought I'd just mention it seeing no one up at the house wanted to talk about it. Not that I thought Luddy would be much help, but if you don't ask you'll never know.

"Saw a cow once that was dead," he said, "drowned."

He was asking for it.

"You should'a seen it, round as a barrel with its legs sticking straight out, rolling round and round," he said, making his hands go round and lolling out his tongue.

I tried to whallop him but he was already at the fence.

"Get off of my property!" I yelled and lobbed a few stones so he'd know it was going to be a very long time before he could come waltzing back with his yabby jar again.

When I was tired of the creek I went back to the house.

"I thought you were going to Egypt," Mrs. Dawson said. "Looks like you crawled there." I was a bit dirty, but not dirty enough for a spanking. "Your mother was looking for you."

"Where'll Grandma be from now on?" I asked.

Mrs Dawson went on kneading the dough, squeezing and rolling, folding it quickly to stop the edges drying out. She wasn't a Catholic. Maybe she wouldn't say where you go when you die because everybody except Catholics goes straight to Hell and they don't like to think about it.

"You know perfectly well where."

I was right, she didn't. She balled up the pastry, slapped it flat on the table and began again using her knuckles.

"Why can't I go to the church? I went at Christmas."

She wasn't in the mood. I hung around anyway, waiting, watching her bake. After a while Mama came into the kitchen to see the clock. It was almost time to get ready for the funeral. Aunt Grace had been ready since the crack of dawn; I knew because I'd seen her walking around the garden all dressed up in her black things. From a distance she looked like a hole burnt out of the air.

At first Mama didn't see me, or she really thought I had run away to Egypt, or she was too tired from arguing with Aunt Grace over selling the farm. That, or she'd just forgot.

"Mrs Dawson," she started to say.

Then she saw me: "Oh there you are Carolyn, I've been looking everywhere for you! You really must stop running off like that—as if I didn't have enough on my mind without you adding to the worry." I was hoping and hoping she wasn't really mad at me, because of Egypt and running away, and maybe she wouldn't notice the mud. I pinched the back of my hand to make myself keep quiet while she finished going over the refreshments with Mrs. Dawson. Time was running out.

"It's all so sudden," Mama sighed, "I don't know how a person is expected to cope." Mama looked like crumpled leaves blown against a fence, standing up only because there was something behind her.

"Good Lord, child, look at those knees!"

Now I was sorry I hadn't listened to Mrs. Dawson and washed my knees like she said. Still, there was nothing else for it but to jump right in and ask, it was my last chance:

"Please Mama, please can I come too—please?"

She looked at me as if someone else had turned up in my shoes; another daughter who didn't know she was supposed to shut up asking to go to places that were too much of a strain.

"We'll see," she said kind of doubtful.

She is always saying "we'll see" as if something will happen out of the blue and everything will change and nothing will be the same as before. It must be hard to be Mama and not be sure of a single thing.

I tried to think of what to say that would show her I was big enough and that I hadn't meant it about Egypt.

"Please Mama."

She was working out how tall I was.

"Carolyn we've been over it before, I happen to think you're too young for funerals dear . . ."

"Please Mama."

I tried to make my face look right, thinking of all the reasons why she ought to let me go: I grew three inches since I was seven, I would scrub my knees, I would wear the good dress I got last birthday, I would behave myself, I knew my Catechism, I loved Grandma, I did, I did. Please. Now was the worst moment, like a rabbit sitting in the road with the headlights getting closer and closer and the rabbit wondering whether to run or sit. The car was either on my side of the road or the other. Please the other side, please.

"Mama . . ?"

She closed her eyes for a minute thinking or resting. She was tired and had almost given up.

"Then for heaven's sake get ready, though Lord knows you won't understand a thing."

The car drove slowly along the dirt road to the church. I kept my eyes fixed on outside the window. I was thin enough not to take up much room, you hardly knew I was there. Aunt Grace drove. Mama sat in the back. I looked over once and there was a tear she didn't notice creeping along her chin. Nobody spoke, not even to tell me to remember to behave myself as if I didn't know the difference between a church and a haystack. I sat on my hands to keep them still and kept my eyes fixed on the telephone poles, the stubs of wheat, the shadows full of sheep, birds on dead trees far away, fence posts flashing by—one, two . . . ninety . . . two hundred . . .

St. Jude's Catholic Church was on a side road but I thought they should have put it near the Post Office in the center of town, next to the War Memorial and the Botanical Gardens so people would know where it was instead of having to ask. It was no place for a church in the middle of some old weatherboard houses and vacant lots full of broken bottles and rusty wire. There was a group standing around outside waiting for us to come before they could go in—Mrs Darcy and Mrs O'Malley in hats and their best dresses, Mr and Mrs Gillard, the whole parish, chatting away and having the time of their lives, good as the Picnic Races. They cut it out when they saw it was us, and put on long faces. Mama got out of the car and walked round to go up the church steps. I opened my door just enough to squeeze out and hurried alongside her so they would see I was part of the family. You could tell Mama was trying to remember how I got there. She couldn't send me back, so I said nothing but held my handkerchief tight in my pocket. I wanted to pull it out to show her I'd remembered.

My shoes felt tight. It was hot.

Aunt Grace rushed into the church as if there was a prize for sitting down first like in Musical Chairs. I came down the aisle with Mama, keeping my eyes low and acting respectful. Inside, the music was so soft you hardly noticed it, dark quiet music like the inside of the church or under the peppercorns in the morning. It wasn't all the music, only the long full bits that go underneath—the real music would go on top, like ripples on the surface with the creek flowing under. We sat up front. I didn't want to be staring at the casket, but it was beautiful polished wood with flowers shining and candles all around. The music began. Father O'Leary came in. We stood up for him and the altar boys, and for Grandma and Mama and me.

"Let us pray. . ."

I didn't forget a single thing during Mass. I watched Mama and Grace and stood up when they did, sat down when they did, and thought of God and Grandma and the dead lambs that got left in the paddock until there was nothing left but a few bits of wool and bone the crows didn't want and I hoped it wouldn't feel like that for Grandma.

"Lamb of God, who taketh away the sins of the world . . ."

". . . Grant her eternal rest . . ."

I thought of Egypt and the Pyramids, and the soft little leather pouch of coins Grandpa had got from there during the War, and how Grandma had given them to me so I could keep them and go to Egypt for her when I grew up. I remembered how Pharaoh took everything he needed for after he was dead, and had it all buried right there with him.

Grandma had nothing with her, only her best dress and the mother-of-pearl brooch.

In the speech, Father O'Leary didn't ask for donations for the Missions like he did at Christmas. I thought it wouldn't be fair for God to want Grandma and donations all at once. Father talked about God loving Grandma and wanting her with Him and how we mustn't mind giving her back but Mama had been crying. She'd been crying hard for two days because nobody was expecting it when Grandma was taken, and because of the farm and the bills and Mama said it wasn't fair that Grandma had just gone like that and left us for ever. To me it felt like Grandma had run away and no one knew where or why. But Father O'Leary was saying we had Grandma for lends, not for keeps. Now she belonged with God again.

It was all right when you said it like that, as clear as finding a secret message. Suddenly I knew: Grandma was gone, but it was like when you take some water from the creek and pour it back again later, the way it blends perfectly and doesn't look different from the rest. You can't tell which is the exact water that was in your jar, but you know it is there. It belongs like it used to only now it's part of something bigger and more important.

Suddenly everything was clean and sharp, like the sky when the drought breaks after weeks and weeks and you had been thinking it would never rain again.

All the time, Mama was reading the parts we had to say in the book, and Aunt Grace was pretending she didn't have to, but when it was time to stand for the last hymn Mama was too tired to get up. She sat there a minute thinking of something else and missed all the first part of "The Lord is my Shepherd." Myra Davis came from behind and whispered to Mama and then Mrs. Davis and Grace began to pull at Mama, holding her up and dragging her between them down the aisle and out the door. Mama could hardly walk and I thought she would rather be in the shade than outside on the porch, but Mrs. Davis and Grace had decided for her. I sat there a while in the cool and the dark with just the candles alight and the end of the song. The men in the suits were getting ready to take Grandma away so I followed everyone outside. There was a crowd around Mama, it was a wonder she could breathe with all the people hanging over her, like a bunch of old crows picking round the last waterhole. Grace was near the big car, talking to the man from the Heavenly Rest Funeral Home.

"It's been too much of a shock for you Maise," Mrs Gillard was saying to Mama. "She was too young to go sudden like that."

"The ways of the Lord are a mystery to us all," said Mrs O'Malley.

"Ours is not to wonder why . . ." someone else said.

"It's the way of all flesh," Mrs. Gillard said because she had read it somewhere.

"Leaving you with all the worry," said another woman, who was forcing Mama to stay sitting on the bench. "It's a crying shame with the price of wool what it is."

"Don't look like rain neither . . ." a man said just to make it worse.

It was a wall of people between Mama and me. I squashed through. Mama was surprised to see me.

"There you are Carolyn," she said, tired, as if she had been searching. She looked around the faces in the circle and then at where she figured I was. Sometimes she just didn't see you for looking.

"Oh dear, who will get you home?"

"But I want to be with you!" I said.

I had my handkerchief to give her. The clean one.

"Nonsense child, your mother is in no condition to worry about you." Aunt Grace was there with her sharp fingers. "Come along now and don't make it any more difficult than it already is."

Some busybody was offering to get rid of me for her.

"No thank you Amy, Myra Davies of the Ladies Auxilliary will go back with her. Mr. Willis from the Home has kindly offered to drive them. It's all arranged."

I pulled away to give Mama the hanky, but Aunt Grace had a grip.

"Carolyn," she said sounding kind and holding tighter, "you're upset—I told her mother it would be too much strain on an eight-year-old." Aunt Grace was using me to push her way through the crowd. "Far too young I said, and I'll say it again. One minute she wants to run away to Egypt, and the next she's making a nuisance of herself."

The ladies stared at me. Their eyes looked at me as if I had been the devil himself in a cotton frock. Their faces said, "Here is the girl who up and left her mother to run away to Egypt." Mrs. Gillard looked at me amazed; they were all amazed. I felt my shame begin to burn on the ground around my feet and rush up and over me like I was a tree on fire that would burn forever.

"That was before the church!" I screamed. "I didn't go—I came back!" My voice came out very loud because it wasn't fair. I wanted to get to Mama. The people acted stunned. Grace looked at me hard, the tip of her tongue between her teeth. I looked back just as hard. She wouldn't dare smack me in front of the church, but you never know.

"It's expecting too much of children. They don't understand," someone was saying.

"I s'pose you shouldn't wonder there'll be tantrums."

Some lady was being nice to me, like I was two years old. "Go along home like a good girl and forget all about it."

I hadn't run away and left Mama. I hadn't done anything.

I was hoping Mama would tell them, but she didn't. I couldn't even see her for people being angry with me.

"Carolyn, I won't say it again," Aunt Grace said and I think I started to cry. I didn't want to be bundled off like an old umbrella nobody wants, but there was no hope of making anybody understand. Grace and Mrs. Davis rushed me towards a thick man in a black suit. He had the engine of the car already running.

"Here she is Mr. Willis," Aunt Grace said, holding me out at arm's length like I was a dangerous animal you could catch something from. "Best get her home," she said. She sounded like the Vet when one of the ewes has to be put down because it's half dead anyway, sort of satisfied and let's get on with the job. She stretched her lips over her teeth at Mrs. Davis and said, "Thank you Myra dear, the child's over-indulged in my opinion, but who's to interfere?" and went back up the church steps to tackle the crowd.

Mrs Davis fussed and the man Mr. Willis opened the door for us and took his cigarette out of his mouth. He held it in his thumb and first finger with the burning end turned in. There was a bit of tobacco on his tongue he spit out.

"Well come along now little lassie," he said, "let's get you home to your . . ." He couldn't say "mother" like he began to, so he had to say "to your place" instead.

Casa la Matta

Zia Linda's hands, brown as grapevines, held a heel of bread as though it were a thing unknown. Her aprons went round twice. Her flanks emptied. It's still a war, she said when they tried to tell her that Antonio had nothing to do with the war, that they don't send military trainees to war. It's my son, she said. "Mio figlio." Zia Linda moved food around her plate. She pushed fava beans here and there the way thoughts slip round in a circle. She scraped congealed things gone cold into the feed-bucket. She washed the dishes in the plastic basin, as if expecting to see Antonio's black hair floating on the surface among the scrapings and the spent lettuce leaves.

She stopped digging the vegetable garden, which reminded her of a graveyard, and padded about in slippers. Her workboots dried out by the door. She went as far as the stoop to toss scraps to the hens, but her heart wasn't in it. The hens stopped laying. There were no eggs for the Christmas *pizza dolce*. There were no more holidays.

Zia Linda was wakeful at night. She got used to the silver light of the full moon, the raven-light of the new moon. Her eyes took on a patina of carbon. The shadows of her eyes invaded her face, and settled in the valleys below her cheekbones. She prowled by the pattern of moonswell, beyond the confines of sleep.

In the village by the sea, her sister, Zia Nilda, wrung her hands and went on pilgrimages to women who had certain powers because her Antonio, known as Antonio of Sperlonga to differentiate him from his cousin, Antonio of Monticelli, had taken to locking himself in his room and refusing to speak. Zia Nilda took her post by the door and begged. She threaded words through the keyhole—

prayers, threats, promises. She worked the lock with hairpins. So that when the door remained stone-mute, she began to travel round the villages looking for the wolfish women with the power. The neighbours called the priest, who came and went away defiant.

Zia Nilda became fine and white as the bleached sheets beaten by the washerwomen on the rocks down at the quay. She cooked eels for Christmas Eve, she braised chickens, fried artichokes, boiled turnip greens to feed her husband. She lived on one strong black coffee with two sugars a day, and waited. At night, she sat by the Capodimonte lamp and fingered the relics and the scraps of paper in little leather bags she kept tucked down the front of her dress. She padded herself with magic.

And it was through her that it started to rain. She called up all the tears of the world to bathe her gritty eyes and dissolve the walls that shut in her son. Water gurgled in gutters and spattered the whitewash. The neighbors wondered behind her back when it rained for a month. She bore the burden of broken axles and cars bogged in mud, the havoc it played with the fishing-cycle, the ruined feast-days, the rusted wheat. She endured her neighbors' unkind thoughts and dark looks hurled on her doorstep like spit.

Her son unlocked the door one day and announced that he was going to take a train up to cousin Bartolomeo in Bonn, where he would work as a waiter.

Zia Nilda accompanied him to the station the day he left, having taken up his silence where he'd left it like a coat thrown on the floor, slipping her thin arms into the sleeves and turning the collar up around her ears so she could not hear the rush of the last big rain that washed out the tracks after the train had passed. It rained out of season this one last time, and when it stopped, the village gossips took it to mean that she had lost her son for good. And they smiled with spite behind the Persian blinds, later, when she took to catching the bus to Monticelli once a week.

By the end of the same winter, the mother of Zia Linda and Zia Nilda, Nonna Assunta, began to fade with the hard frosts. She kept herself company talking to the rabbit-cages in the cowshed. Waiting.

Then she began waiting by herself in bed. The farmhouse returned slowly to the wild. The stones fell from the walls, the tiles from the roof. Nonna Assunta kept her own wildness to herself, a wrinkle in the big white bed. They had trouble combing her hair when they laid her out.

Weeks after she died, and after the villagers began calling the place Casa La Matta—House of the Mad, an iron lock appeared on the door now belonging to Zia Linda and Zia Nilda. Before the lock, furniture had started to disappear. There was a shadow-rectangle of faded paint on the wall where the carved chest had stood. The land around the house was good, as everybody knew. But unlike bed-steads and night-tables with chamber-pots and wash-stands and rush-seated chairs, coffee-grinders, and the iron pots from the hearth, unlike the coffers for grain in the attic, and the bent forks in the drawers of the dresser, the land belonging to the house was nailed down.

So when the villagers had quickly laid the lingering spirit of Nonna Assunta to rest and had seen to most of her belongings, the daughters retaliated with a lock against the outside world and un-spoken plans against each other. They agreed the house was half each, and that was all they agreed on.

Zia Nilda set a kitchen chair in the hallway of her house and pondered the small and vacant room of her son. She decided that Antonio of Sperlonga would come home to be married if she gave him somewhere decent to live.

Zia Linda begged the postman in vain when there were no more letters from the barracks, and thought of setting out to search for him, but it was too far north. Besides, she knew the terrible truth she admitted to no-one—Antonio of Monticelli was dead.

So they rolled up their sleeves and tackled Casa La Matta—Zia Linda in grief for her dead son; Zia Nilda full of hope for hers.

Zia Linda went at night. She found where the wood-doves roosted on the rafters under the hole in the roof-tiles, which she widened to facilitate their passage. She observed that they came and went at dusk, settling for the night, head-tucked, at about the time Orion set through the attic window looking west. In the pale light of stars she began gathering all the loose stones that had tumbled from the outside walls. The cairn rose steadily in the threshing-yard.

Zia Nilda began her weekly practice of catching the rural bus from outside the fishmonger's and traveling an hour on the back-road to Monticelli. At the Saturday markets she bargained sharp-eyed and down-to-the-penny for plates and cups, peelers and sheets, saucepans and buckets—a mirror-household to her own, fit for a newly-wed. She stood at the bus-stop in a nest of plastic bags.

On her first trip, however, she paid the extra fare and continued past Monticelli and on to Pontecorvo, to the silversmith's, where she bought a hand-tooled silver heart, the closest she could find to what she wanted, although she had no intention whatsoever of taking it to the church and hanging it there with the other *ex-voto* with its note saying, "In thanks for favours received." On the way home in the bus, it seemed to be burning a hole in the bottom of her shopping-bag, so she hastened to make an extra trip to the old house next day, where she prised out a loose stone and concealed it in the wall under the bedroom window.

The next night Zia Linda sensed its presence—there! where her night eyes picked out the warm rosy spot in the wall. She was aware of the stealthy stuff it released into the mortar, seeping like venom. She also noticed the cabinets gradually filling and the pieces of furniture that arrived by car on the weekends, and heard the poisoned clang of wedding-bells and the nighttime toll of funeral bells, and she sat at the top of the ladder in the hayloft patterning her thoughts in and out of cupboards like the scurrying feet of nocturnal mice.

She smelled the musk of incense in dark apses, heard the smoky sighs wisping heavenward from the wicks of candles, saw the sullen glint of brass on altars. "I am the Life, Alleluia," the words said. "I am the Light." It was springtime, and Easter.

Next afternoon, she made the hour-long trip on foot to the only shop in the valley, where she bought several eggs. Choosing only spotless white ones, she selected them from the basket and wrapped them herself in a cotton towel to cushion them for the trip home.

On Ash Wednesday, when Zia Nilda came with workmen to have the fireplace ripped out of the kitchen, she found that every light bulb had disappeared from all the rooms of Casa La Matta, and an egg had been placed in the centre of the floor directly under each empty light-socket. Gathering the eggs without comment, she dropped them into the well beside the vineyard. The well was covered with a rattling sheet of tin, because its deep circle of water was afloat with opalescent green patches—lily pads of contaminating verdigris copper used to spray vines.

An electric stove was circled in the catalogue, and the thick oak mantel torn out of the kitchen wall under Zia Nilda's approving and watchful eye—the ashy flagstones prised up, the sooty throat of the hearth bricked up like a tomb. The place in the wall healed slowly from its scab of fresh plaster. But the new paint, blue to waist-high with whitewash above, was barely dry when Zia Nilda noticed the heavy wooden dresser had been dragged out of its place in the corner and set right in the middle of the wall. At first, she ignored it, and that it always stood open, always empty. Later, she ignored the cheap but sturdy lock when it appeared across its doors, a finger laid on lips.

When she had gathered all the stones that were lying about among the brambles, Zia Linda began to scavenge loose ones from the walls. Then she began transporting them inside one by one, and set them in a row.

Zia Nilda plodded up the road in the late morning and discovered the line of stones forming on the floor across the middle of the kitchen. As the number of stones increased, certain little things began to disappear—the lids to the saucepans, the forks from the cutlery-drawer, every second pillow-case she had hand-edged with crotchet. Zia Nilda shook the dresser on its squat wooden legs to see if it rattled. She mopped at muddy footprints on the floor. The row of stones increased steadily. Finally, she summoned back the bricklayer and had a permanent wall erected in its place, right through the centre of the room. She looked at the grey cement drying slowly in patches, sour-smelling, wet-rag smelling, and laid a hand on the dry place in the centre. It was a wall that meant business.

The east half of Casa La Matta ripened steadily like the wheat pulsing with sun in the fields, filled with juice like the grapes distilling sunlight on the vines. Zia Nilda came on Wednesdays bountiful with gifts, wearing a flush of blood under her skin like a bride. She baked in the oven and supervised painters. The walls smelt of sugar cakes and purple, fennel cakes and yellow. She lay across the handwoven sheets in the master bedroom, and her heart unfolded, like the wings of a moth.

Tender summer leaves canopied the west half of Casa La Matta, whispering night-chants.

In the course of her ranging, Zia Linda sought out the source of the spring at the place where the eddies had sculpted deep pockets among the willows trailing in the shallows, where the water twined in dark curls pinned back with the silver flick of fish. She found safe footings among a treachery of rabbit warrens pocking the pale grass on the slope downhill. She found the skeleton of a fox in its fraying blanket of fur, and the carapaces of beetles. She cut willow fronds, stripped and dried them, burnt them black to charcoal over simmering night-fires. She bundled willow sticks, cut beech boughs, piled roof tiles. She built a seat of tiles and branches by the window in the attic, where the midsummer night tumbled in turquoise, swirling up again and out through the bare dark rafters.

One by one, she moved stones from the yard where the workmen had piled them.

In the attic, she observed the path of Orion and kept track with charcoal, plotting the tilt of his belt on the wall. The soil in the vineyard crazed, leaves wilted before their time, grass turned to paper. On Wednesdays, Zia Nilda, with her eyes unaccustomed to the rhythms of the country, noticed none of this. So the summer advanced, nights blue as quartzite, dragonflies dipping on a mirror-still pool.

One evening in mid-autumn, Zia Nilda arrived to find the front door draped in black crepe. She tore it down and hurled it into the well, where it billowed and settled like a bilious cloud. She found the bed festooned with twine and feathers and a coverlet of straw. She found jars out of cupboards, pillows tumbled, canisters empty, twigs in the drawers. On the table set for a party, a cake made of mud amidst garlands of pondweed.

That night, she let herself into the other half of the house. It smelled of wheat-sacks and wet leaves and fresh blue mildew, and she found herself standing among maps in shifting patterns of moonlight cast through rafters and the overhanging trees. She saw where the moon's long nails had picked at locks, scraped on shutters, spilt sugar, sowed dusty green mould in the bread. Where it had blasted the vegetables tumbled in the winter bins. She heard the metallic sound of its stomping on the red iron staircase grafted onto the wall outside—the din that kept Zia Linda awake. Chipped paint covered the walls with the shapes of things seen from the corner of the eye. The roof had rearranged itself on the floor in tall stacks of tiles. The dresser stood beetle-browed in the middle of the room. She found a rock and smashed in its doors. By unsettled candle-light her fingers pried among splinters, poked among the magpie-jumble and tore off the ribbon binding sheaves of letters tied together tight around the middle. Each envelope bore the same address in her sister's unschooled hand. Each was postmarked Monticelli, Province of Frosinone. Zia Nilda tore them open—one . . . twelve . . . twenty—to find neatly-folded sheets of blank paper. She pillaged the dresser and lit a bonfire in the garden, and the smoke swelled black and putrid with burning plastic and buckling aluminium, singed feathers and paper—drifts and drifts of charred paper soaring. She combed every corner for fire-fodder.

At last she stood looking up the ladder to the loft in the rafters, at a bare sky unsettling.

From the rocks at the well-spring, Zia Linda smiled at the yellow leap of firelight at the foot of the slope. As she worked, she saw Orion topple slowly to the brink of the world with his cudgel and his bearskin, drawing behind him a pall of cloud.

At the top of the ladder Zia Nilda put out her hands to feel for a footing. The floor smelt of insects tunneling, dry-rot gnawing, timbers splintering. The half-light filled with pattering and feather-preening, the sounds of leaves slick with rain, dry hide on bone, rain falling like acorns. It rustled with branches and whispered with spiders busy with cobwebs.

Zia Linda tumbled stones, lifted stones, rolled stones aside, un-blocking the spring. She watched first a trickle form, then a gushing, then a jet as thick as her arm, as her waist. The banked-up water surged out of her dam. Zia Linda felt her boots fill with water, water surge round her skirt. She watched first a ribbon descending, then a rivulet, then the river itself descending, bent toward the house.

Her eyes were all darkness with the fox and the wolf, the night-vision of predators, sharp teeth, the stealthy set of the paw, the swoop of dark wings soundless, the rush of the kill. Her eyes were black coals, seeing distant, her hair the wind beneath darkwing hunt-ing. She saw moon and stars and rainwash together, the river roaring into first-light nudging clouds streaked with rain. She stood behind the dawn, the sun in the east, her livid morning a peacock-tail fan-ning over the valley, glinting with moon-ripples, a pall speckled with stars. The valley a smooth lake, a cloud-mirror melting, edge-singed with silver. Her ravenous morning lapped the horizon, meeting the Hunter finally descending.

She rose up from the water, from the stones on the hillside, her mind riddled with moonlight, three stars in her belt.

SHATTERED

Dinner plates, salad plates, soup plates, cups and saucers, a coffee pot and tea set belonging to an exquisite replica of a 17th Century Richard Ginori dinner service for twenty-four at a couple of hundred dollars a plate, and another service for twelve, more modern, decorated with fish, also Ginori.

I move on to dust the second shelf.

The dinner set I designed and marketed nationwide in the States, again with fish but hand-decorated by an artist with exhibitions to his credit and made in hand-thrown Italian pottery in a village in Umbria. A sushi set. French lion-handled consomme' cups, a tureen that stands eighteen inches high with claw feet and a putto on the lid. A stack of platters of all sizes, in ceramic, some decorated, most of them plain white.

I remember the name of a shop in Rome—la Porcellana Bianca. Sure was. White china and lots of it, a feast, a really dangerous place. I wish I'd thought of that—the sheer elegance of a shop that sells white only.

I keep dusting. It's like a damn shop in this kitchen.

My sister is in the middle of telling me about her day at work with the emotionally unstable and says that one of her charges is violent. If you turn your back to him he will attack you. Today he tried to punch her out and she'd had to grab his raised fist and tell him not to fuckin' think of touching her. Later, the same guy came sidling up to her and said,

"Jesus was killed by the Romans.

He was born in a sandcastle with his mouth slit."

Her amazement at the bizarreness of this is something I can't participate in fully. I keep dusting. She presses me to acknowledge that it is a most spun-out goddam awful thing to say. It's really not all that shocking to me; I say I could have achieved a similar result by writing out various disjointed phrases and pasting them randomly together.

She still reckons I should work in one of the Houses so that I can hear real-life weird stuff like that and use it in my writing. I point out that if I listen to her regularly, I can have the weird stuff for my writing without having to change diapers on adults over six feet tall who want to bash me.

I know nothing. The violent ones don't wear diapers. Mostly, they are just looking for a chance to bash you.

She is going back north soon. Her Francis is building the photography studio for her while she's away. He's so wonderful he makes me sick; they both make me sick.

A removal van pulls up in front of the house and I recognize the name on the side through the acacia fronds and know what it is. The driver comes to the door and I wasn't expecting them to ever appear, let alone today, so I am not welcoming. They back the truck down the driveway and start unloading crates of stuff I haven't seen for six years. I go inside seething. The driver comes back with the clipboard and the delivery receipt and drives off. I wouldn't say so to his face, but this driver would never have made it into the United Parcel Service Delivery-Man Pin-Up Calendar someone told me they have come out with in the States. That one I believe. Yep, I could see that. I always said that the UPS vans were the sexiest things on four wheels, and they are—dark chocolate brown you can almost taste.

My sister is belligerently cheerful and says that if I unpack one box a day it'll be done in no time. And no time is exactly what I have to deal with the leftovers from an old divorce settlement I have nowhere to put. She is impatient with my lassitude over unpacking the crates. Like our father, she is a Hands-On NOW Person and they both drive me crazy. "Do it now and it will be out of the way"—

that sort of thing—said usually right in the middle of another task. I notice, however, that the crate with the chandelier is not in the consignment. There is no furniture either. Just cardboard boxes. A box a day, my foot.

My sister is in her element this afternoon. She trims my hair and I am disgusted to see she knows how to hold the swatches flat between the first and middle fingers as the pros do. She pins up the top hair and starts at the underlayers, levelling, going on to the next layer, levelling. I am being forced to read out an article she saw in the *Weekend Sydney Morning Herald* about a writer who is seeing the Shrink-to-the-great-minds-of-our-time in New York and who is told that the key is that nobody cares. The writer is nit-picking in his mind about the hour he has spent there, the hole in his bank account, and was that the result of half a century of presiding over the psyches of a major moment in cultural history? He leaves in vague disappointment, gathering up the little mound of angst over every word, the struggle for every sentence, from where he set it on the desk in the office, clutching it back to his breast under his coat as he leaves. I read on and follow him into the cab, where he is grumbling that his great-aunt Hannah could have told him that.

"But the point," I comment, "is that she wouldn't, and even if she did, coming from her it wouldn't mean a thing."

In a flash of enlightenment, he comes to see the point. I read, "That's right! No-one cares! People have troubles of their own! It's okay. That doesn't mean that you shouldn't do it; it means you should do it, somehow, for its own sake, without illusions. Just write, just live, and don't care too much yourself. No-one cares. It's just banter."

That's what she wanted me to see, the word 'banter.'

"Banter! Don't you love that?"

She takes the word in her teeth and gives it a shake, wags her tail in terrier-glee. I don't point out that calling my craft 'banter' is like telling her that all she does is 'take snaps.'

We talk about her new place in Northern New South Wales and she describes the seven metre-by-four metre studio, drags out snapshots (I notice Francis is wearing knee-high gumboots against the ticks and leeches, it's the rainy season) and tells me that the flies there are so big and so lazy that she has a field day swatting them. Her eyes shine.

"I used to leave the door open, you know," she tells me. "Let the bastards in and then swat away for an hour at a time. I hate the brutes."

Perhaps she has a unique point of view on her power within the universe.

She leaves. It's 1:00am, but I start on a new piece. It was in the back of my head all afternoon and I own my time now in the quiet place in the dead of night that I seem to inhabit best. I set down the first words of a short story, in the full knowledge that no one cares.

The story is going back to my life in Rome, and at the end of the stint I see that I have the equivalent of an hour's fly-swatting to my credit. It's going to be a good story. My editor in the States emails me to say he wants me to organize the order of the stories for the collection when I send it. He also sends me a note in Magyar.

I tell him, "That is not a language, it's a throat disease."

I tell him, "Idiot."

I sleep a few hours and am up again at 5:00am to get back to the story. The crate-mountain outside in the carport glowers through the wall and I ignore it until it starts chanting a dirge that drowns out all other sound. There is no other sound, actually, just the odd birdcall disjointed among the trees. Mohammed in pyjamas summoned, I square off in front of the mountain.

I read the markings—'kitchen china,' 'attic bedroom,' 'main b'-room,' 'books.' All also marked 'CP'– Carrier Packed. I have no idea what is in most of them, I wasn't there six years ago. I go inside for the Stanley knife to slash the tape on the top of the first one. I tell myself one-at-a-time will do it. One sucker a day.

Oh well, at least I have learned that nothing marked 'attic' or 'basement' is worth opening, I could ditch the lot intact and still sleep peacefully. Peripheral spaces tend to accumulate junk. Maybe

I'm realizing some sort of repercussion of yesterday's idea that 'no-one cares.' If no one cares, what's the point of accumulating words so that they're just piling up all around?

I go back to the streets of Rome (I worried to my editor that people wouldn't like seeing the dire little place I am talking about, and he said never fear, Italy is a tarnished dream, the others fret about them joining the European Monetary Union.) My toe hurts a lot, I need to have it looked at, it's quite swollen—you can bet I won't go barefoot in the rockery at night any more. I put the broken toe into the story; the character is someone who is slightly damaged. I work on. The morning is almost gone. I realize I have drifted off-track; I have gone wandering the streets of Rome, past the nightlit shops, stepping into the wash of gold on the sidewalk, contemplating past wrongs.

I get up to make tea and pass the painting hanging in the hall that my sister gave me. I remember what she said when she gave it to me, pointing out that the canvas is patched. She said it was highly appropriate as a gift to me because it and I are both slightly damaged. Still, I figure she and I have one thing in common—we are both tenaciously attached to the idea that it's not all over yet. The article last night mentioned that old age is a series of lurches rather than a gradual decline. I reckon we're braced.

She comes back here to take away the projector I found in the pile outside. Within the fifteen minutes she has been in this house she has received three phone calls, made appointments to see two old friends, checked up on her shifts at work and I wonder how people seem to know exactly where to find her at any given point in time. She tells me she had lunch with a friend, also a writer, and told him straight to his face that his work is self-indulgent. He asked her how she knows this and she replied that she just does. The Oracle is In; She Knows.

She asks me if another friend, Camille, can stay here for a few days. Camille likes it to be known that she is lactose-intolerant and a vegan, and drifts around your kitchen absently rearranging things, asking you if you think a certain slight aquaintance might be vegetarian. She is always dismayed when they aren't. Last time she stayed here, she was at the store every five minutes getting 'supplies' to appease the constant hunger that is with her. She nibbles all day. My sister says the girl needs a goddam feed of steak. I suspect indeed that Camille's tender green spirit inhabits the frame of a voracious red meat eater. I say sure, Camille can stay, but warn her I'm writing and don't want to be disturbed.

I call my mother and tell her I unearthed a forgotten cache of hand-painted pottery. She sells it on my behalf to her friends at half retail. I calculate that the proceeds will keep me for a week or so and I won't have to look for a job right now. And there's always the Lautrec lithograph I can sell if I need some cash to tide me over.

Camille arrives with a backpack and a box of tissues. She is recouperating from a shattering love-affair. Turns out this one was with the woman she and her boyfriend shared. Camille has left both of them. I think, far out! She hands me the sheaf of bills she collected from the mailbox at the top of the drive. She looks at me and sighs gently, proffering also her pain. I take just the bills.

"Thanks Camille."

My share of her grief is left firmly on the doorstep.

Apparently her own house is awash with manly tears and uninhabitable.

Suddenly Camille's spurned lover starts to visit. She has been kindly given my address by her husband, who was abandoned for Camille. I smell bubbling pots of mischief a-brewing. She and Camille lock themselves in the guest bedroom just to talk. The joint boyfriend learns of this and visits also. My house feels like Grand Central Station. At dinner-times they cook vegetarian food in the kitchen—subdued at first, with bare subsistence in mind, later collectively, joyfully. Over the days one or another of the three appears grinning in the door of the studio with a plate of dun-coloured food that I refuse. I consider asking them to continue to talk together by all means, but could they do it while unpacking the boxes to help me out, but decide against it. The damned stuff has to be sorted. It has been sitting there for a month and I leave it there. It's mostly the worthless kitchen crockery. I have become used to using the good stuff.

The now-reinstated spurned lover turns the tables and threatens to leave Camille and the boyfriend. I hear them pleading with her and then long silky silences where I figure they are trying to convince her in other ways. Camille and the boyfriend come to the door of the studio like puppies dragging along the threadbare three-way relationship as if it were a bit of blanket. They wonder if I have a minute to talk? I look up from the computer and they backtrack quickly—maybe later? I am aware that the lover comes and goes at odd hours, that Camille sniffles a lot and goes about the house despondent. The lover's friendly husband comes to the house looking for her, also just to talk. I know she happens to be in. I walk down the hall and ask through the door if she wants to see him. Apparently not.

I try phoning my sister. I am the only one in the universe who does not know where to find her instantly. I am finally successful and tell her what's going on here. I need her to talk to the three-ring circus that has pitched camp under my roof. She says she can't right now, she has a one-on-one charge today. She tells me to just march in and lay down the law. I remind her that this is not one of my stronger points, and that they are her friends after all.

She arrives, bristling, with her charge in tow, an enormous young man with Down's Syndrome, who wears a floppy cricket-hat and clutches a potted geranium. She has managed to convince them at work that this is an Outing. She is not amused. The lover's husband is suddenly a shape in the open door, knocking soundlessly on the wall, apologetic, interrupting again to ask if I would mind seeing if his wife will speak to him.

My sister says "For God's SAKE!" and goes to tell her to get her butt straight out here and talk to the man.

"Go outside!" she tells them and they scamper out. They argue, he cries, he leaves.

The wife comes back into my house fully reinstated as lover-defiant. The guest room door closes with a soft click. I am quite satisfied that I have made my point that this whole thing is preposterous. I need my sister to go in to them and say something. She does. They will leave. Tomorrow. Promise. My sister and her charge leave. I am suddenly very hungry.

"For Christ's sake!" I shout over them.

Camille and the boyfriend are clinging to one another behind the kitchen counter. The lover is purple in the face yelling obscenities at them.

Yes! She is leaving them—both of them goddammit!

Yes! She won't take being treated this way.

I try to suggest that we all respect the fact that she wants to leave and that she is always free to go, no one is stopping her. She turns on me, wild-eyed. I have no idea how she heard me over her own shouting.

"No one cares!" she shrieks and reaches for a plate off the shelf and hurls it at Camille.

"Shit-faced little veggie bitch! You tell her!" she screams at me.

I say it is far from me to tell Camille anything of the sort. I try to step in sideways between her and the china-cabinet. Someone has called the husband who shows up in time to duck a slew of dishes. He hides around the corner of the door. The lover is beside herself, the crashing china feeding the blood-frenzy.

I step up to her and she turns on me, the tip of her tongue between her teeth. She makes a fist and I grab her arm, just below the elbow, and wrench.

"Don't even fuckin' think of touching me," I say evenly.

I am standing in the middle of the floor crunchy with broken crockery, stunningly, gloriously amazed at myself.

I say, "Now get the bloody hell out of here, all of you. I want my house back," and walk into the studio, closing the door.

I sit in the leather chair and let the pale blue light of the monitor hum over me as I read the screen. Car engines start outside the house. This latest piece is proving more challenging. I see myself reflected in the studio window, as though I were in my own pale blue underwater world. I recognize myself, sitting at the computer, at the end of my finances, having to decide if I can work on the story-collection only at night. I could call the Gallery, see if they want me to come back . . .

My editor emails a note saying that one of the stories will be published elsewhere as well, the one I wrote six months ago to the only person I have ever loved. I think of the words 'no one cares.' I accept that I am doing this because I secretly hope that someone actually does.

If not, it makes no sense.

LACEY

"Grant him eternal rest," the man in the long black dress and funny hat said.

The big pile of dirt beside the hole was baking hard in the sun and the flowers were browning around the edges like ruffly white eggs frying. She would like to put that hat on after all, but Nell had left it at home.

Nell had said: "An hour in the sun without it won't kill her. It'll teach her not to spoil her clothes." Caroline had her hat on. "You angel," Nell had said about Caroline, but not about her. "You see what you done to this hat, you bad girl? God'll send you straight to Hell."

Now she wanted to go back and get it but it was too late, and the man in the black dress was looking at her, like she was supposed to be saying something. "The Lord is my shepherd . . ." he was saying.

She knew that one. "Amen," she said aloud, alone against the pulsing sound of him and the flies together.

Nell shook her arm: "Hussshhh!"

". . . there is nothing I shall want. . ." the man said. The buzzing hung in the air over the open hole as if she could see the words drifting through the shimmery-grass in the paddock. The still figures seemed to move as if seen through squiggles of white heat, the air hung out like white sheets, wavery like over candle-flame.

She looked down into the ground. They had put the box in there and then it was gone. Gone, she thought, all gone.

—It was always dark. He said: "Don't tell nobody, you hear?"

"Amen." they all said and she was back with them and they walked over to the house, only her and Nell: the others went to the church hall. Only her and Nell back to the house but not Caroline.

"We better keep them two kids apart till things settle down," Henry had said.

Then Nell put her in the ironed white bed but she wanted to come down.

The floor was cool under her bare feet.

"You get yourself right back to your room," Nell said. "You stop that snivelling, you hear?"

She could feel the breeze around her ankles, touching the hem of her nightgown to the back of her legs. It was outside.

"You hear me?"

"You know she don't like it in the dark alone," Henry said. "She won't sleep without Caroline." She wiped her sleeve across her eyes. She had not seen Henry where he was outside the screen door. Henry's voice blew in from off the porch where the curly rocking-chair was. She pressed her face to the fly-screen and could see his shape a bit lighter than the dark around.

"No, you ain't going outside," Nell said. "Get back to bed."

Henry's chair creaked.

"Lacey, let go this minute."

But she fit her whole fist around the handle of the screen door and held on, tight and kept on holding against Henry's pulling and Nell's pulling her away from it, them both together. Tight.

"Let go or you won't come to town tomorrow," Nell said.

"If I was you I'd leave it awhile before I went taking her to them lawyers," Henry said.

"No harm in letting them see what's best for the child," Nell said.

"You take her there tomorrow and there's no telling what she'll come out with," Henry was saying.

"You want ice-cream tomorrow? You want it or not?" Nell said with her face so close she could feel the breath. "At Cole's?"

There was starting to be a picture of Cole's Cafe and of her sitting on the trolley-car with white gloves on. She wiped her mouth on her cuff and let go a little so Nell could undo her fingers from the handle and turn her round to face the stairs.

". . . chocolate?" Nell was saying. "Chocolate and vanilla if you're a good girl, two kinds."

Henry went out.

"But you have to go to bed now," Nell said.

The good seats weren't taken so she could sit by the window. It was all windows. Nell said "Sit!" Nell was pulling her skirt over her knees. "You sit still, you hear me?"

—He said: "You lie still, you hear me?"

She let herself sway with the trolley-car. There was a lady looking at her, holding a purse with two hands on her knees pressed hard together, tight. The trolley began to tick and clack. She felt it go from side to side rocking her too, as if the hard wooden seats were a boat. It felt nice with closed eyes, like on the river or the swing. She opened her eyes and saw that the lady's eyes were like nails and she wondered why the lady was looking at her unless it was because of the ticket. She crunched it tight in her hand and pushed it into the pocket of her overalls.

Nell would get mad. "You know what happens to people who lose their ticket? The man comes and makes them get off and walk."

No walking, she thought and closed her eyes so that the blue man would hurry up and come and get it and the lady couldn't take it before he did. He'll get mad, she thought.

"Don't touch!" she said aloud with her eyes closed. She opened her eyes again and the lady wasn't looking any more. The lady was looking out the window. She had a tight little mouth on. Once there had been a lady on the trolley with a crackly brown paper bag of round pink candies in her purse, but this was not the same one.

She didn't want to leave Cole's. She jangled the glass with her long spoon and picked up with both hands and licked the white sweet cream and the chocolate bits from the edge. Nell took it away from her and gave her two pointy wafers to hold in her hand and then they went to the other place, but she didn't like it there.

"You, Lacey," Nell said. "You sit still."

There was a man in dark clothes sitting down and glasses like Henry's. The glasses, not the clothes.

"I'm warning you," Nell had said outside the glass door with the gold writing. "If you don't sit still in this here office you can't come home on the trolley. You want to be left here by yourself so you can't get home?"

Nell said to the man, "Our late uncle was her guardian."

The man had a red pencil and big yellow paper.

"Do you mind if I give her one of these pencils?" Nell said. "With slow kids like her you have to keep them busy."

It was a red and a blue pencil, both.

"Now you stay hushed, Lacey dear," Nell said.

He was talking.

Nell was talking.

"No, not exactly a blood relative, he was her guardian—her dad and him was together in the war—old war buddies." Nell squared her bag on her knees like the lady on the trolley. "The father didn't have much to leave her, you understand, but it takes care of her keep."

There was red and blue on the yellow paper.

The man was drawing too.

But Nell was telling!

She remembered it was Nell had said: "You keep away from that barn, you hear me?" But now she was telling.

"It was a terrible accident, it was over before we even knew he was in there. The while place went up in five minutes flat, the barn you understand. Fire."

The barn smelled of hay.

The yellow paper was tearing, but it was the pencil, not her; it was the pencil making long cuts in the paper like a stick in the dirt.

"You, Lacey, stop that right now."

Nell took the pencil away.

Nell had turned into black and yellow strips. The light was coming through the window cut up with scissors; everything was in black and yellow strips.

Except the man's eyes were two circles of white fire, flashing at her.

"My husband and I would be willing to keep her," Nell said.

Coming home was in the dark, and the windows of the trolley-car sent her back her own face instead of letting her look out. She pressed into the glass and then she could see out again. It tasted cold. She could see the street lights like fast candles in the dark. She could hear the lampposts flit by: *Fftt, Fftt.* After a while the stores flew away and after a while more, there were no stores and then there was nothing to see. She closed her eyes letting the trolley sway her, like Caroline's hammock where they played house in the barn. The dark smelled of hay.

It was too dark in there so she opened her eyes again.

It was Nell had said: "You two stay clear of the barn. He's probably in there sleeping it off. You can play, but stay close to the house."

But then Caroline and her were crawling through the part of the wall where the wood was a hole and she caught her sleeve on the teeth and Caroline was angry: "Shuttup, you big baby!" she said. "You wanna wake up that old drunk?"

The dress was torn.

"Shuttup, will you?"

But Nell would be mad: "You take care of these clothes because it's the last stitch I'm going to buy you. You can go naked for the rest of your life as far as I care. You hear?"

"Will you stop blubbering?" Caroline put her hand in her pocket. "Here, hold this. Only it's not for keeps, okay?" Caroline went back into the hole in the barn wall. "You gotta give it back, mind, it's only for lends."

Now the dress didn't matter. She opened her hand to see the marble. It was a cat's eye, yellow and green. Inside was a caught fish. She closed it in her fist; she didn't put it in her mouth. "Not for eating," she said.

"Why you want to go eating that, when we got cake right here? You want to sing Happy Birthday? You wanna play that?" Caroline said. "Now shush up or you can't come."

It was dark. They went along with their knees on the hay.

"Cut out dawdling willya, come on. What's the matter with you anyway? You want a birthday or not?"

She could hear he was asleep.

—He said "it's all right, I won't hurt you . . ."

"See? Told you he's asleep. He can't bother no one."

—He said: "Now just lie still like a good girl and let me have a feel." And then it used to be his cold trembly fish hands under her dress and him holding her with his wet mouth. "Just one little feel."

But now he was asleep. All quiet, all right. Quiet, quiet, shhh.

—He said, "Just one. Now don't you go telling no one, you hear?"

Happy Birthday to you.

It was dark and smelled of hay.

Caroline had the matches.

The trolley stopped and Henry was waiting up and Nell sat her down at the table and made bread and milk. Red jam and warm milk.

"Lawyer said there's nothing we can do," Nell said. "He says Bunny was the guardian and now he's dead we have to let her go."

"Did he say there's any chance we can get custody?"

"You, Lacey!" Nell said. "Get your fingers out of your food."

There was jam on her fingers. She licked it off.

"God, will you just look at her," Nell was saying.

Henry went out onto the verandah: she heard the door squeak.

Nell was always saying, "Close the door or you'll have the place full of flies. Close the damn door!"

Nell took the plate away.

Henry's voice floated in and up to the light in the kitchen. Moths were banging around it. She rested her cheek on the table and watched the moths batting against the bulb. It was all right, the light was hot but it didn't hurt them.

"It was good while it lasted," Henry was saying outside.

"Fifty dollars a week," Nell said. "Sure going to miss it."

DIVING TOO LONG

Edie's mother stood in the back porch shouting as if the two men were miles away, not at the end of the yard, where Edie sat sucking a strand of hair and watching them mow the back paddock before it got so dry the whole place went up.

"Hello? You men," her mother called through the screen door, "Excuse me, Mr. Day!"

She never looks at you, Edie thought, you might as well not exist. She mightn't see you, but she's seeing something out there. Whatever it was, it was far, far, away, farther than the boundary of the yard, farther than the rusty little farms and towns with one pub, the roadstop cafes, the petrol stations, unused railway stations, volunteer fire stations, bus stops and post offices, a single unwavering line of sight that passed by everything, like the river flowing down to the sea.

But Edie knew that unlike the river, once her mother reached the shore she would have to stop. Edie saw her standing at the edge: long, curved, and white, with her thin back hunched in her baggy print suit and one frightened toe tasting the water as if she was afraid of being swallowed whole.

But that wasn't Edie. In fact, she had just been telling the John Days that the sea was her real home and that she was probably adopted. At night she still felt the lull of waves and remembered the dip of the Southern Cross into the horizon like a plunging kite.

On the back porch, her mother's line of sight skipped John Day and Johnny Day and skimmed the back fence.

She called, "If you don't mind, I need a hand inside. The washer's jumping."

Johnny Day went up to the house; young John stayed.

"How come you're both called John Day the same?" Edie asked.

"You want me to show you what you gotta do to be a boxer?" John said. "Because that's what I'm going to be."

He unwrapped the newspaper round his lunch and held the double page out at arm's length. "You crumple it with one hand, and when you finished one page, you do the next and the next, till you done the whole thing. Tip I got from this boxer bloke Dad knows. Terrific for the biceps."

Flexing, he made her feel.

She wiped off the hard feel of his cotton sleeve on her shorts.

"You ever had tadpoles?" he said.

"Tons," she said. "What about you?"

"Nope," he said. "You live on the road you can't. They slop."

Out of water, they died, even the ones getting legs.

Edie slid off the lawn chair and tested the Cyclone gate for squeaks. She took the oil can they were using on the mower and oiled the hinges until it swung out fat and slick with grease. When the Days were gone, she would wedge her toes under the loose bit at the bottom and hang over the top and swing in slow, heavy arcs, waiting. From the gate you could see the road from town.

"You know that girl in the place with the weird roof like this? Girl name of Gail Woods? Well, she still believes in Santa," Edie said. "What a joke."

John looked sideways from under his long greased curl.

"She's so dumb." Edie said. "You know what she called her cat? 'Whitey'. And her budgies? 'Greenie' and 'Yellowie'."

She almost spat but shook her head instead.

"Poor things," she said. "My dog had a good name at least."

John Day scanned the yard. "So where's the dog?"

"Dead."

"So how come a little kid like you stopped believing in Santa?"

She put her fists on her hips and rolled her eyes.

"You gotta be joking, it's been years! I'm ten next birthday you know. Besides, I saw." She set one foot at an angle to the other and folded her arms. "If you don't believe me I'll show you."

She made him follow her around the garage to a pile of cartons stacked against the workshop wall.

"See that hole up there? Well, I climbed up and looked in, and I found out."

She walked back to the mower.

"I could of gotten killed you know. I fell and practically died. I got this scar." She fingered a long pale crescent at the base of her neck. "I had to have sticking plaster it bled that much. But I saw him making that stove and then I got it for Christmas. So he lied."

"It's not the same thing," John said. "What did you call your dog?"

"Chippo," she said, "Full name was 'Mr. Chips'. So why isn't it the same? It's either the truth or it's a lie."

"No it's not," he said. "I can see why a bloke would lie about that. Instead of making your kids miss out on Santa Claus, you lie. I spose you wish you'd never got all those presents?"

"It was still a big lie."

"So? You were a big snoop."

She touched the scar. "Anyway, I think 'Whitey' is a stupid name for a cat, specially because it's white."

"Your Dad used to make stuff?"

"There's a whole shedful of tools, but they're locked up. My Mum's got no use for tools she said."

"C'n I've a look?"

"No, it's illegal."

"What do you mean illegal?"

"My Mum said."

"How can it be illegal?"

"Certain stuff you can't touch until they decide what to do with it. If you do, it's illegal. Anyway, you're not allowed to."

He balanced the screwdriver Edie's mother had lent them on his palm.

"This one of your Dad's? Number three Phillips head?"

She nodded.

"My dad's got a whole box of these out in the car. Lined up in order of size."

"Mine too. On pegboard so you can reach down which one you need."

John Day squatted and tipped the mower back by the handle to show the sharp blades clotted with grass like matted hair. He steadied it with his boot and yanked the nylon cord. It sputtered short of starting.

"You aren't supposed to do that without your dad," she said.

"So what? I use these things all the time. Fuel them up and all. Tank's right there."

She came closer to look where he pointed. It was a screw cap all right.

"That where the petrol goes?"

"Course."

He picked up a rectangular can with 'Shell' on it and sloshed the bottom.

"You ever lit a fire?"

She backed off.

"You want to?"

"I promised Mum not to mess around with matches," she said.

"So who said you need matches?" He closed his fist and flicked the air with his thumb. "Got a lighter in the caravan."

"Your Dad'll catch us and we'll cop it."

"Wouldn't be using matches so it wouldn't count."

She stared at the toe of her shoe. There was a small ragged scuff. She licked her thumb and plastered the flap back in place but it didn't stick.

"My Dad lets me do what I like," he said. "We have camp fires all the time."

She didn't stop to think. "So what? My Dad let me drive."

And she could see it again, her and her father sitting on the front seat the day they dumped the Falcon.

Her mother had yelled from the porch, "Get rid of that damned thing before the child kills herself playing round it."

And he did it.

He'd lain still for a while thinking it over with his eyes closed against the sun. Then he got up from the lawn chair and squared off in front of the car.

"You driving?" he'd said to Edie.

She was seven, eight, it was ages ago.

It was the first real day of summer, hot and bright (she remembered squinting up at his face to see if he meant it about her driving), with millions of flies the size of pinheads trying out their new wings by flying blind crazy up your nose. She sat on his knee behind the wheel and he said, "First put on the brake . . ." and she'd pressed against the instep of his boot with the toe of her runner, "Pull the gear stick towards you, take it in your palm with your hand open, gentle, it's not a club. . ." and she'd taken the lever across her palm like he said, not grabbing but in control, and pulled forward and up, ". . . it's an H, slide it along the bar of the H . . . that's it, now let her go."

They let out the handbrake and slid in neutral down the river path, the whitewalls popping stones on the loose gravel. They rolled to a stop among the feathery leaves under that clump of peppercorns at the end. The branches trailed like weeping mermaid hair over the windshield or like seaweed hanging down complete with bunches of small pink underwater grapes.

He and Edie sat side by side on the front seat listening to the whine of insect wings and the warm muddy slide of the river and the sudden buzz and whir of cicadas that stopped suddenly, as if someone was turning them on and off, and maybe she and her dad were remembering trips starting out while it was still night to make good time before morning, with a bed made up in the back for Edie, and she remembered driving along in the dark and seeing the telephone poles stringing out the wires ahead of them and snatching them back again along the road they left behind, racing down to the coast, and her falling asleep staring at the space between her parents sitting black like tin cut-outs up front, and the sudden trees leaping into the sweep of the headlights beyond.

Then her Dad had sighed and said, "Well, I hope that'll satisfy your mother."

And they'd walked back to the house and left the car there.

"She was a beaut in her day," he'd said.

Under the peppercorns that Saturday she had run her finger along the white flash on the Falcon's side and sworn that as soon as she could reach the pedals she'd practise driving that car, so one day she'd stroll down the path with the three keys swinging on the keyring round her finger, a circle like a chant—ignition, glovebox, boot—and she'd start her up and drive her right out of there along the old airport road, past Alastair McCechnie's place and the Tom Blamey Pub, up the Tumbarumba Road and keep on going with her elbow out the window and her eyes on the road. She'd grown out of two sets of shorts since then, but she must have forgotten to measure if her feet reached. Last time she went down there, the seats were blurry with yellow pollen and dried peppercorn petals as if it was some old ghost car that came upholstered in pale pink moths' wings.

"I got a 1966 XP Falcon," she said.

"Where!" John Day said.

"Hereabouts on our place."

"Let's have a look!"

"Hang on," she said, "You don't just get to walk up and have a look for nothing. First you got to deserve it."

"Whaddya mean first I got to *deserve* it!"

She folded her arms and planted her feet.

"How do I know I can trust you?" she said.

Johnny Day Senior came down the back steps and called,

"C'mon son, we got work to do."

"She says they got a '66 Falcon convertible. Wanna take a look?"

Young John turned from his father to her, trying to pin her down, but she turned and strolled off across the yard.

Maybe later, her back said.

Later, her slow walk said, maybe, maybe not . . . Depends.

"Aren't you ready?" her mother said. "He'll be here shortly."

"He never comes, so why bother."

"Well this time he will, just wait and see."

"Yeah, I bet. Besides, I got stuff to do."

Her mother scraped the peanut butter crusts into the bin. She took her foot off the pedal and the jaws closed. Even the rubbish gets peanut butter for lunch, Edie thought. At the end of the yard, the Days were finishing too, she watched through the venetian blind. Staring into the broad sunlight drained the colour out so the Days looked like a picture in a magazine left out in the rain. The heat changed the edges of things. She heard the bark of a sheep, the bleat of a crow.

She went back to her room, knowing it was useless. Sometimes she swung on the gate, or walked along the path, one step for each stone along one side and one each stone back. The same thing every time. Wait, wait, wait. The path was edged with snapdragons wilting in the heat. She wondered why her mother bothered, they never lasted past Christmas, those frilly cut-out edges and soft colors like paintings. At first they were pretty, but then they went brown.

Wait and wait; wait, wait, wait.

She lay on the end of her bed, legs dangling, waiting.

Time dragged.

That was why she had invented ways to change it, to make it stop so she wouldn't notice. One way was to freeze things in the moment: a shadow on the wall; the smell of cut hay; a shovel rattling in the bed of a passing ute; Hank Williams on a radio moaning through the gyprock wall; the threat of rain nudging clouds over the sun; the brown edges curling on those stupid dying flowers; the phone. She was the only girl she knew had to keep on playing Statues with her life.

But the best way was to shut her eyes and hold her breath as long as possible. In her mind, she watched herself step up to the edge of the pool and take a deep gulp of air like she was diving for something way down the bottom, a twinkling star glinting on the dark blue underwater sky like a coin and she saw herself plunge and follow the pale greenish-white tips of her fingers stretched out ahead turning crinkly from too long in the water, but it was always deeper than it seemed from back there at the edge, clinging with her toes before casting herself forward, and as she was lying there on her bed imagining it, her chest squeezed and she felt herself come up gasping, surprised that her face had broken the water and her mouth had opened by itself. She remembered how shocked she was to find that no matter how close she felt she'd come, she hadn't drowned.

Her eyes snapped open as the clammy wave receded and left her lying damp but still breathing on the chenille spread, and she suddenly understood something: if she was waiting for the phone to ring so she'd know he wasn't coming, and she was dreading it would ring and it did ring, that would be bad, right? But now that she thought about it, even if it rang at the very last minute, and she was really disappointed, it was still a lot better than the times she was left waiting and waiting, sitting around like a dope taking care not to mess up her dress and then having to change out of her good clothes after all, and go to the kitchen barefoot on the cold black and white lino and get something out of the Frigidaire, and the old fridge would sort of jump, kick back to life like it was surprised to see her still there when she was meant to be out for dinner with her father and there they would sit—the two of them in silence—her and Mumma picking at whatever it was without caring, Mumma not saying a word, and Edie already in her pajamas, wriggling her bare feet under the table to get off the stray crumbs that were stuck to the soles, and then because there was no time left and it was bedtime anyway, going back to her room and straight to sleep and all because he didn't care about anyone or what it felt like.

She rubbed the wiggly pattern the chenille had pressed into her cheek and decided to go back outside and find the John Days before they left, because it didn't matter if she was ready or not, her father wouldn't come, not this time, not any time, and it was better to get on with it and give up. She was never going to go to bed like that again, not knowing why he hadn't shown up until the phone rang (sometimes later that evening, sometimes next day) and her mother spoke into the receiver in a low private voice but with an edge, and she lay under the blankets squeezing her eyes shut and plunging into the dark tangle of weeds sliding along her sides and tickling the soles of her passing feet as she slipped through sharp and deeper than a shaft of light. And in the last moment before she fell asleep she'd realize she'd been diving too long because of the rawness on the bottom of her toes from the gritty cement edge of the pool.

Getting up from the bed she caught the flash of her own reflection in an angle of mirror. And suddenly, because it seemed like such an easy thing to do, and because she finally recognized it as a thing that was already there, already real, a thing she was always catching glimpses of out of the corner of her eye, she went ahead and did it: she killed off her Dad.

Why not? she thought. He isn't real any more anyway, only a voice on the phone. He never came, only phoned. That John Day was always saying "did your dad used to this?" and "did your dad used to that?" It was the way they talked about him used to this and used to that. It was never what he did now. She didn't even know what he did now. So why drag him around with her today, tomorrow, carrying him around her neck like a dead weight, like a man who had drowned?

She kicked off her good shoes at the end of her bed and almost ran to look for John Day. She already had the story ready.

"We found him afterwards, but it was too late," she said. She waited for tears, bright drops in brimming pools. "It was last year . . ." she said with lowered eyes, ". . . with the drill and the storm and all. Electrocuted to death." She could taste a fizz of tears, real ones. "So that makes me almost an orphan."

"Well," John Day Jr. said. "Not to be mean or anything, but everyone knows that's kind of a dumb thing to do. My dad mightn't be the smartest bloke on the block but he'd never do a silly bloody thing like that."

"It was not a silly bloody thing!" she cried. "It was a tragedy!"

She ran. At the top of the river path she turned and screamed at him. Birds lifted.

"I hate you John Day!"

The driver's side was almost rusted shut. Chips of flaking chrome stuck to her palm. Red dust grabbed her throat. The upholstery prickled the bare backs of her legs.

That day with him down here. All those little flies.

"She was a beaut in her day," he'd said. "A real beaut."

He'd let her carry the circle of keys: ignition, glovebox, boot.

"I don't know why she's dead set against the bloody car," he'd said. "You'd think she hated a man to care about anything." He'd sat looking at the keys in his hand as if waiting. "Anyway, that's the end of it," he'd said.

She remembered smelling the vanilla of the weeping willow pep-percorn trees and looking through the windshield and the trailing branches and seeing nothing, as if from inside a tent.

"Sad thing is," she remembered him saying, and wondering what he meant, "I don't think she's capable of it herself."

"Go to bloody Hell, John Day," she said with her jaw set so hard her teeth hurt.

But she knew it was her fault, she'd made her father die like that. She could have said he was killed in some war, or in an accident, or drowned saving somebody's baby in the river, but no, she'd been too mean to let him die properly. She'd said he'd died stupid, and now it was too late.

She stared ahead over the dashboard of the car, into the bleak pink landscape of loss and betrayal.

SWEET MY INFANT, BORN TO DIE

When Maria Pia finally wakened from the stony sleep of three days, they cried '*O Jesu-Maria! Un miracolo!*'

And because there had not been a photographer to witness the accident at the time, they sent to Pontecorvo for Beppe Gesualdo and his camera and tripod so that they could honour the custom of presenting the Madonna with a record of the event in gratitude for mercy bestowed.

They staged the scene as it had happened—Maria Pia lying beneath the overturned cart, (this time gazing gravely at the camera) her cousin Antonio steadying the head of the donkey. On this occasion, however, the laden tray of the cart was prudently propped up with stones.

The pilgrimage to the Basilica of Monte Cassino and the Chapel of the Miracles took one full day. The family hung the photograph in a space on the walls crowded with other photographs and paintings and little silver objects in the shape of hearts or legs or arms, which stood for episodes of miraculous escape from death. In the midst of this mosaic of human suffering and gratitude stood the altar bearing the statue of the Mother of Sorrows, as tall as a person, her head bowed under a three-tiered crown, her neck festooned with chains of solid gold and pearls, her bare feet emerging from beneath robes of rich brocade shot with silver thread, her downcast eyes painted weeping in her black, desolate face.

The family of Maria Pia left Monte Cassino haunted. They paused on the way home and filled their troubled stomachs with a banquet of fish and lamb, salad and figs, and as much wine as would wash away the unspeakable whisperings of lingering ghosts—the way peasant women take mops and buckets of a morning to the thresholds of their houses to cleanse them of any dark presence that might have crossed in the night.

But now that they had a photograph in the Chapel of the Miracles to prove it, the family decided they had indeed been touched by a miracle. They went about the village proclaiming it—"*Miracolo!*"

The inhabitants of the valley were eager to recognize that Maria Pia of the Miracle was one of them—that she, at only fourteen years of age, had been elevated above all others. They also realized that perhaps there were benefits to be had.

It began to be said that the Madonna had appeared before her in the roadway, at the window of the farmhouse, in the Chapel of Miracles, and that the dark-faced effigy had wept in her presence. Her mother produced a handkerchief with which it was claimed she had wiped the sacred tears, and small pieces of the cloth were sold, to be kept in tiny glass boxes with gold casings and clasps. Maria Pia was beset by mothers seeking a cure for the croup, by farmers seeking bountiful crops, by brother seeking retribution against brother, by the unrequited lover, by those to whom money was owed. Her intercession was sought in all manner of things both of this world and the next. On Sundays, she was accompanied by her mother and aunt along the cobbled street to the stone church where pious women knelt on the whitewashed steps to kiss the hem of her skirt.

But, reluctantly, the family began to turn supplicants away when they realized that Maria Pia could not effect the miracles required in return for the modest sums of money or other gifts slipped discreetly to her mother. Those who came to see her left hastily and with burning faces when they discovered that although she might not be capable of staying the hand that directed the misfortunes of their lives, she could indeed see into the unlit depths of certain secret places in their hearts. She reminded Lucia D'Amato that her son's eyes held a particular turn of colour that was also remarkable in the eyes of Signor Francesco who lived in the neighbouring farmhouse. She knew how often Compare Melucci visited the widow Cecco. When the roof inexplicably caved in on the abandoned Fondi place she said 'It is because of the sheep'– and her elders remembered Pietro Fondi riding his mule out one night with a shotgun, and they relived discovering his neighbour's slaughtered flock and the sight of Pietro's shattered skull, the dark blood and the pale pink matter of his covetous thoughts spattered on the ground where they had found him in the honeysuckle-scented dawn.

They left her to her reveries and crept about the edges of her presence in the house, uneasy. Maria Pia of the Miracle sat alone by the window wrapped in darkling wings, communing with angels.

Padre Sammartino was not satisfied. He arrived at the house in full ceremonial vestments, preceded by a reluctant altarboy swinging a ciborium. She had little enough to say to him—"Padre," she said, "the key to the parish coffer, that you say is lost, is hidden in a hollow beneath the third stone in the fireplace of your kitchen. And the money buys land, and the wine of that land turns to blood."

It was demanded that her uncle, Zio Crocefisso, whose wealth and prestige far exceeded that of any of his brothers, be called upon to discipline the girl, but she revealed to him a vision in which she had seen him sitting at a table with a secret candle in the kitchen, taking pen and ink to his dead father's will—the body not yet cold on the bed.

Her relatives and neighbours began to fear the traces of the thoughts that crept about the corners of her mouth and avoided meeting the distant contemplation in her eyes. Something began to fester in them, below the surface, a thing that tainted to sourness, like the blight in a bin of winter wheat. The womenfolk no longer took her to the markets, to the village, to the church; she was no longer required to help feed the chickens, tend the sow, fetch the cow from the pasture. But after dark, people began returning to the house, knocking softly at the door, bearing gifts: a bottle of wine, a fine prosciutto, a pungent goat cheese, sausages fat and fragrant with fennel, long braids of dried garlic, lard-studded salami with meat veined like marble. Maria Pia's mother accepted these things through the half-open door, and the visitors went away in the uneasy hope that there would be an end to the deaths of their animals, the bitterness of their wine, the tumbling of walls, the failed crops and the unseasonable fall of snow, thick as the hush around the child at the window. Maria Pia withdrew into silence, closed as a locked door.

There were some—the priest, and her Zio Crocefisso—who did not come secretly offering appeasement. Their separate humiliations joined like the twisting strands of a candle-wick and burned with one flame. If the people of the valley murmured it, these men gave voice to it—Maria Pia of the Miracle had descended like a plague upon the valley, like a scourge.

The whisperings and accusations rubbed against one another like the attrition of stones, until the rougher edges of reluctance and shame were gradually worn away and self-righteousness ground conscience into grains of sand that shifted easily at the fickle ebb and flow of tides. Maria Pia's parents were forced to realize that if their only child remained with them, they would be obliged to sell the farm and leave.

Maria Pia's mother wrapped herself up against the cold and went to the train station to buy a single one-way ticket. She packed Maria Pia's few belongings in a suitcase that she bound with a leather strap. Maria Pia of the Miracle was sent to live with her aunt at the seaside because, as they told her, the change of air would do her good. Also (and this they did not tell her) perhaps her absence would remove from them the burden of responsibility now upon them for every evil turn of fate that occurred. Parents and child said their farewells amidst arid tears and the girl boarded the train, taking her place on a wooden bench in third class. They gave her some cheese and bread for the trip and a little money.

In making arrangements for her stay, nothing had been mentioned to her relatives about the miracle.

In comparison to the house in the country, which dominated the valley like a fortress from its seat among the wheat fields and vine-yards, the apartment by the sea was small. Maria Pia was unused to life at close quarters, where relatives and neighbours lived across landings, up staircases, down staircases, in buildings surrounding the courtyard—a press of people, insistent, demanding—people behind every door. She was unused to the conflicting aromas of bubbling stews, boiling pasta, frying fish and brewing coffee wraithing about her, the sudden silence of the afternoon siesta, the scrape of rush-seated chairs dragged outside and the twilight talk of the women beyond her window where they sat with their needlework, gossiping. She shared a room with two cousins and lay awake at night, the voices of the angels swirling in the tideswell of the teeming world around her.

In December, the goatherds came down from the nearby moun-tains, bringing their songs and their wooden flutes and whining bag-pipes to the piazza and the streets, where they played under the shuttered windows in return for any small charity that might be of-fered them. They sang the lullaby of the pink-and-white Virgin in the village church—"Sweet my Infant, Born to Die." They played in the courtyard where Maria Pia stayed. As she leaned from the bal-cony to place a coin in the hand of the youngest, she saw in his heart the stony days and nights of solitude in the mountains, the music his only voice among the rocks and the goats, and she saw the caper-bushes clinging wild and spiny to the edges of precipices. She saw his gaze follow the effortless plunge of a hunting hawk—the swift dip and swerve that mapped the course of its earthbound prey—and shared his wonder at the mystery of it and the pity.

And as she gazed into his heart it was as if she would take his cold feet in her hands and warm them, offer him the comfort of her voice in the chill nights and days, shelter him from the rain down-pouring, show him ways along the stony paths that even he had not discovered, show him also that there was joy in his solitude because he alone, of all those she knew, was clean, his brow unmarked, his hands unscathed, his spirit windswept. She showed him these others, the people who reached down from balconies flooded with light and the golden sounds of cooking and the rich food-smells of *festa* to offer him a coin, these people wrapped warm in the spaces they had hollowed out in the cupped hand of their God. But she knew also that even as he walked the edges of precipices he was held upon the open palm of God, within His sight. Her gaze told him "Go in peace," for she recognized in him, and therefore in herself, the first work of the Creation. She saw the time before words were bent into lies, before blood was drawn in anger or envy, the time before hearts drew into themselves—closed as stone, dry as husks, the time before passions were given vent and allowed to destroy, and small grievances harboured. In the eyes of the goat-boy she saw the instant when the light had been separated from the darkness, dawn in the mountains.

And so it was Christmastime, and the household was caught up in the flood of endless visitors and preparations—the fetching from the cellar, the carving of the best ham, the breaking of *torrone*, the crackle-crusted loaves of bread, warm and fragrant from the oven, the freshly-killed capon, the joyful wine—the torrent of festivity pausing only briefly over fish and bitter olives on the Vigil, and she was swept along on the surface of it like a small piece of driftwood, unremarked.

Spring came and went, dawn broke earlier. Maria Pia began to wander the streets, coming to rest at midday in the piazza at the highest point of the village, on the steps of the fountain facing the church, her darker shape etched into the blinding whiteness of sun on the bleached stone around her. Eyes watched from behind darkening shutters, as if she were unaware. She in turn watched the comings and goings of strangers who were known to her in dreams.

The Englishwoman, *La Signora Inglesa*, arrived at the beginning of the summer. There was the sudden flush of life in the big house at the edge of the piazza—the linen hung out to air on iron railings at every window of the façade as the house of the *Inglesa* broke into full sail as it did each June. The people of the village watched the ritual unloading of canvases, boxes of pigments redolent of solvent and linseed, her sketchbooks and the folding canvas stool she took with her when she drew from life in the village, the huge wooden easel crusted with years of spattered paint. The iron-hinged doors stood briefly open, were closed again, and the village returned briefly to the rippleless flow of its every day.

And because the fishmonger was an uncle of Maria Pia, and because the Signora Englishwoman mentioned it to him first, and because her uncle had no daughters of his own, Maria Pia was chosen to be sent to the big house to help *La Signora Inglesa* with the cleaning and the errands, the cooking and the washing. It was agreed among her relatives that her board and wages would constitute suitable recompense for the expense they had incurred in housing and feeding her. It had not gone without comment that her own parents visited ever more infrequently, wrote rarely, and sent money never.

Her first day at the house of *L'Inglesa* passed uneasy—from the first minutes scented with coffee thickened with sugar to the last stroke of the broom and the taste in her mouth of long-settled dust disturbed. She swept and polished, washed floors, folded linen, laid out tubes of evil-smelling paint carefully—in rows, as instructed—and helped move the easel to the place in the room where the light fell gentle in the morning but safe from its acid noontime bite. She arranged provisions, rinsed dishes, aired rooms that had been lying fallow. As night fell on the first day on which she was to earn her keep in return for such work, she retired early to her small room in the big house, restless.

Like herself, the Englishwoman tended towards silence, her unuttered thoughts retreating to an inner place where they gathered and sank as if into sand. The first time she caught Maria Pia watching her prepare to paint, the Englishwoman told her that painting was like capturing the soul of a thing, that it was very serious work, work of the spirit, and that she must never, never be disturbed in this work unless she herself requested it. Her painting consumed the hours of the day, during which the Englishwoman remained at her easel, stopping only to eat at midday and to rest a little before recommencing once the edge was gone off the sun. She and Maria Pia sat opposite one another at the small table in the kitchen and the English-woman either probed and scooped at the pith of what she was attempting to capture in a painting, describing it in words, or remained silent, with that same struggle of words and images churning in her mind.

Days passed, roses bloomed in the garden of the big house at the edge of the piazza, fish followed their swirling course into the nets stretched out to snare them, the sun came into its power, setting red and fearsome at night, and in moments stolen from her work, Maria Pia quietly witnessed the paintings rise from nothing.

She watched in wonder as the charcoal took its first sweeps, blocking out forms on the white canvases. The blocks became solid planes of colour interlocked. The houses and shops came into being, re-created as if in bricks and mortar, solid. She paused in her washing and bed-making, marvelling that a brush might create a wheel of cheese, its smooth compact paste; the liquid glint of wine in a glass; the strew of crumbs from a loaf of bread standing brittle by the yellow shape of a pear she could almost put her hands around; the piazza standing silent with the heat reverberating from the granite flagstones; the view beyond the window, battered sails scudding on the cloud-punctuated dawn.

But there was no painting done on the increasingly frequent weekends when the Englishwoman played hostess to her friends from Rome. "*Magari*" the villagers said in envy as they watched the house flow with milk and honey. It was observed that the evenings at the big house lasted until the first trawlers put out to sea just before sunrise. The *signori* came to the house but they did not arrive with other travellers on the dusty bus that wandered the coastline down from the capital, nor did they arrive in wagons or donkey-carts; the friends of the *Inglesa* arrived in powerful cars that blocked the narrow streets and they sat lazy in the garden under the pergola laden with grapevines and roses. From the kitchen, Maria Pia listened to her mistress speaking in accented Italian with its vowels clipped like the hedges that surrounded fields in a far-off place, where the houses nestled together in comfortable huddles among fields of gold. On these occasions, it seemed as though everything

the Englishwoman touched had turned to gold—she spread sump-
tuous suppers in honour of the people from the City, who picked
politely at their food, sipped from fine wineglasses and spat olive-
pits delicately onto the prongs of silver forks. They were never shown
the work in the studio, however, which remained locked, and Maria
Pia was dumbly resentful of this because she found a degree of comfort in observing the slow act of creation that occurred before her
eyes, so when the Englishwoman was content to draw lighthearted
sketches to amuse the company, Maria Pia rankled inwardly.

The festivities at the house of the *Inglesa* accumulated in the village consciousness. It was Ferruccio La Spina, proprietor of Caffe'
l'Isola, who wiped his hands on a linen cloth behind the counter
and began to wonder, aloud, what the silent girl saw up at the house
that pulsed with exotic life like a greenhouse of orchids. He mentioned his concerns along with the espresso coffee in the morning,
and served them up at night along with the brandy.

"Foreigners!" he spat, "That's who is to blame if we never get
ahead—*povera Italia!*"

And if Tommaso Capidoglio stopped by to dust the flour from
his arms and sip at a small vase-shaped glass of sambucca at eleven,
there were plenty of others willing to ask what the *Inglesa* actually
did with the profits from the pictures she made at their expense. As
the baker said, squinting with his good eye, but seeing with the one
whose iris was as white as crushed wheat and just as opaque—"After
all, it is our faces and our village she sells to make her living."

"Worse than that," said Signora La Spina, "it is my impression
that the *Inglesa* is teaching the child the bad habits of the city."

The other women, gathering for the evening summary of each
day in the courtyard, pressed Maria Pia's aunt for news of her niece,
although she vowed she had none. They commented on the numer-
ous sleek and polished men who came to the house from the city,
their tanned, close-shaven faces, their manicured hands. They commented on the peacock clothes of the city-women.

"Not even God Himself could have invented such colours for
the hair of a Christian!"

"Ah," said Teresa Vallanzana, "*La nostra piccola Maria Pia la vede lunga e la dice corta,*" although they were ignorant of exactly what she saw, as what she said was next to nothing. It was speculated that her tender green spirit must surely be compromised, that such goings-on up at the big house must test her innate sense of right and wrong. It was agreed that only simple folk such as themselves could tell the difference.

The villagers began to look sideways at Maria Pia when they encountered her on her daily errands. The shopkeepers provided food and drink on credit to feed the people who came from the City, and were trapped in their own impatience with foreign ways, which rotated daily in a bitter circle around the pivot of their need.

Maria Pia herself owed none of them a lira, but she was forced to accept scraps of paper listing various amounts of money owed to the *tabacchaio*, the baker, the butcher, and the suppliers of wine and oil and fish—those who slept at night dreaming of the promise of a time to come, a time after the lean—a time of plenty, when the *Inglesa* would come to their shops and *botteghe* and settle her accounts.

In the time of lean, however, they spoke disparagingly and aloud in the presence of her housemaid, whose eyes were lowered and whose face burned, and who did not acknowledge what she was intended to hear—that promises of much money flowed about the streets of the village like so much water, and that like water, it was as difficult to grasp. "Ah yes," they said, "it is the way of the world – the rich people, the *Signori*, live like kings without scruple on the backs of the poor."

So although the Englishwoman made sure that Maria Pia was adequately clothed and shod, it was as though the girl found herself standing barefoot and outcast on the polished concrete floor of the wine merchant's shop with a shame that was not her own clutched about her like a ragged shawl. She bore the wine-merchant's jibes about outstanding accounts, returning always to the house accompanied by a delivery-boy bearing extravagant provisions and yet another crate of wine which would stand empty by morning when the *stranieri* were there. The wine and food evaporated into words she did not understand and shone dully in the eyes of the guests when they woke next morning, late, calling for coffee and fresh towels, complaining about the din of the early Saturday markets in the piazza below, and about the clangour of churchbells on a Sunday morning.

Maria Pia's voice wedged in her throat like a fishbone, like her humiliation. She remembered hard times in the country, when she and her parents had sat down to an evening meal of bread mounded with fried onions rather than go a-begging credit in the village. She swept, tidied, and made up beds at all hours of the day in silence. And so it was that she, used to setting the tasks of daily life in order according to the pattern of the sun, was borne along like a skiff adrift through the days when the household swelled with people and she was called upon to do things out of sequence. It was as though the sun and moon had been shifted from their dominant roles in the order of things. She came into her own true silence only once the last vehicle had left and the stillness had settled again about the rooms and she was free to open the windows to admit the air familiar with the fresh tinge of salt. She watched the stale miasma seep out of the walls as though the place were being scrubbed clean as the sand of the beach by the breezes lifting the curtains.

On the Monday mornings once the *stranieri* had returned from whence they came, the Englishwoman rose late, bedraggled with sleeplessness and the sour aftertaste of too much wine and returned to work on her paintings—at first with the shutters closed against the clear light of mid-morning, and then more wakefully, more intently, as the glasses of hot coffee did their work and she was slowly restored.

It was the portraits in particular which fascinated Maria Pia once the faces of those who sat for the *Inglesa* took form and shape. Flesh built up quickly, pasty strokes that were smoothed and burnished, and before her very eyes, there, on a flat white surface, came the pulse of life—the Widow Santolina, her eyes lowered in mourning beneath heavy lids; the merchants and fishermen, mirror-images of the lives evolving in the streets and houses of the village, filling and emptying over time like the moon.

And like the moon, the work of the Englishwoman was at times as sharp as a scythe, glimpsing something of the souls of those who sat for her, and at other times she worked languidly, content to float above the horizon, mellow, bestowing her rich golden light on the unworthy. Maria Pia saw the exchange of smiles and polite words at the end of each sitting, the unctuous praise and the imperious acceptance of it, and she knew that beneath it all burned deep resentment, other words and thoughts that were spoken in the light of day and that were never presented in the half-light of the studio, as one would never offer a basket of cankered fruit. Maria Pia suffered her burden of silence, conscious of the fact that the light of the sun would not necessarily dispel the darkness of bitter hearts and that the gentle moon did not grant peace.

On the August night of the Feast of the Assumption, a part of her sleep broke away from the heart of her like the shell of a walnut and she rose from her narrow bed and entered the studio, to stand contemplating the fresh paint, the colours now altered in the white sweep of moonlight, the sheen of linseed oil like a mist of dew on the faces of the people whose eyes looked into hers in effigy. As if in a dream, she removed one of the brushes from its place in a jar, and touched the bristles to the pools of colour laid out on the palette. To the portrait of Pietro Luna the fisherman she added a green stripe from the centre of the forehead to the jut of his chin, sealing the thin lips behind their secret. In an unschooled hand, she wrote across the bottom of the picture *Naufrago*.

To the picture of the piazza she added a black drape around the door of the wine merchant's house, and wrote the name *Luisa* and the word *caduta*. A path of moonlight spilled across the sea and in through the open window to lie beneath her naked feet as she went from painting to painting.

In the morning, the *Inglesa* opened the door of the studio to find her work disfigured. Hurling back the covers from the sleeping girl, the Englishwoman screamed, "*Villana!*" and dragged her into the studio, shaking her from the dead sleep of night to show her what she had done. Every image had been defiled with a new colour, every picture scrawled across with the letters that had formed so effortlessly under Maria Pia's hand, the colour flowing as easily as blood in the veins, as the thread of a story.

Weeping and terrified, Maria Pia touched the fresher paint over fresh paint, tracing with her fingertip the words that she had written, discovering them, speaking them as she went from one picture to another.

"*Naufrago,*" she said, "is sinking a ship for the insurance money."

One by one, she approached the canvases, following with her finger the words she had written on them, and like the stations of the cross she passed from one to the next in succession—a disclosed Via Crucis; the red dribble of blood flowing from the serene fountain in the piazza, and the name of the woman who had died there, her throat slashed with a knife, she and her unborn child found dead in the open one still morning, the name of her husband, *Savio Macchi,* written beneath hers. Here was the wine merchant's shop and its shuttered window, now draped crudely in black, the colour of the heart of a man whose door had closed forever to his child, and she traced the word *Caduta* and said, "She is dead on the streets of Napoli."

The faces of the people who went tranquil about their business each day had been tinged with the colours of their souls—green for envy and avarice, black for murder, yellow painted around the eyes of the rosy-faced Giuseppina Cavalari, whose husband kept his shotgun loaded and the door locked, sensing the neglect of her duty in the cold bed she shared with him, the reluctant offering of her body to him, and her image smiled from secret corners of the full mouth on the canvas, the name of her lover scrawled in red across her bosom.

The *Inglesa,* incredulous, watched the girl proceed around the walls, stopping before each picture, naming the unspeakable passions and crimes she had incised into each one. Maria Pia fell to her knees at the end of it, weeping. The *Inglesa* dragged her back to her room and left her.

The aunt and uncle did not know what to do with the *Signora Inglesa* when she pounded on their door that morning; they offered her a glass of strong black coffee which was brushed aside in fury, and no, they did not know what demon would enter the head of the child to make her do such a thing, and no, they did not know who was going to recompense the *Inglesa* for the work of months, completely destroyed. "She is no child of ours," they pleaded, "we are not responsible." And the tiny apartment shrank into itself, cringing into the narrowness of its poverty and its cramped quarters with too many people and suddenly there was no longer room to accommodate the brooding, dark soul of the niece sent to them inexplicably from across the mountains. The *Signora Inglesa* stood, refusing to sit, refusing to be treated with hospitality, aware of all this, yet demanding all the same that they come to take Maria Pia away. The Englishwoman insisted that they come immediately to witness the destruction the girl had wrought, and meekly they followed her, walking along the road behind her, in the thin light of a penniless morning, defenceless under the burden of a blood-tie they now wished to deny.

They begged to be permitted to summon the priest, whose house was along the way. Don Gesualdo was roused from his daily *Matins*, sitting as he was at his scrubbed table praying over coffee. He chose a purple stola from among those black and white and green. He kissed the fringe of his vestment, and placing it around his neck, and agreed to accompany them.

By the time they reached the house, however, they found that Maria Pia had taken the canvases and had stood them side by side around the walls of the villa, transforming the place into a public display hitherto shrouded. The *Inglesa* approached through a press of people who turned eyes of fire on her and spat at her feet despite her denials. Don Gesualdo, confessor to the village, stood transfixed, deafened by the words he read which screamed loud into the morning the things he had heard whispered in the secret sanctity of the twilit box where he dispensed conventional penance. He fell to his knees and closed his eyes and ears to the bedlam, invoking the Virgin.

Carlo Treccani, who had sent his pregnant daughter Luisa away, turned the picture of his shop to the wall, and with his boot smashed the wooden stretchers, crushing accusation as if it were a straw. Maria Pia stood at the centre of the crowd, unseeing, unhearing as the paintings were taken up and hurled to the ground, trampled, smashed. They demanded that she be taken immediately to the church and cast to the righteous wrath of God.

Maria Pia stood still in the face of the wild voices and the shaking of fists, of the hands that threatened to clutch at her and tear at her eyes, her hair, and Giuseppina Cavalari gathered to herself the fury of the crowd and struck her across the face, almost knocking her to the ground. They all turned away from the litany of wrongs hitherto kept secret, and closed in upon her, desperate. She stood dumb, surrounded by men come from their work, mothers with babies on their hips, women who had abandoned wicker baskets they had taken out to fill with meat and fish and innocent bread and the ripe flesh of tomatoes, tender new lettuces. Fruit spilled among the mangled canvases, and rolled about the ground slimy with paint and the taste of bitterness. Maria Pia found herself forced back against the walls of the villa garden, where she stood defiant under a cascade of roses overhanging the girdle of stone. The crowd pressed in around her, uncertain as yet of the place to which their rage and dismay was to lead them. Treccani spat in her face and she raised her hand to wipe it, as if to defend herself. With one voice, the mob called for her to be exorcised.

Her aunt and uncle hung about the edges of the mass, uncertain, conscious of their own children safe at home, of the abandoned morning coffee turning cold on the table in the kitchen, of the long nights of visiting and being visited, the harmless gossip in the courtyard, the grapes hanging placid in the garden beyond the well-swept stoop. The aunt thought of the washing on the lines strung crisscross in the courtyard, adrift in patterns like sails—handspun white sheets bleaching in the noonday sun against the cobalt sky, and began to weep.

Maria Pia felt the hatred of the crowd surge toward her, and like the breakwater at the quay, waited for the waves to smash boats unanchored against her. At first she said nothing, but stared individually into the faces around her. The sky turned violet, streaked with the gathering power of the sun, the black shadows of the broad leaves of the fig-tree patterned the wall, the roses hung heavy, releasing their scent above her head

When she spoke, she said only, "I have done nothing. It is you who have done this. It is you who have done these things. These things are no sins of mine."

The boats in the harbour rocked uncertain in the gentle swell of waves, the artichokes stood full and compact among their spiny leaves in the fields, a tangle of fish swerved as a body against the mother-of-pearl pebbles lying undisturbed by the tide. The priest forced a path through the press of bodies, confronting her where she stood, a dark-eyed child in a bower of roses. Invoking the saints to cleanse her, they would take her to the church.

But she was far from them, high in the mountains, watching for signs of rain, following the rise and fall of sudden squalls lifting to negotiate the higher places, the drenching downpour. She was at once the hawk swooping, the flight of the hare, the roots clinging to desperate pockets of soil accumulated in crevices, the fall of a stone. Her body stiffened as they bore a crown of thorny saltbush towards her, and she looked down at them from her place on the summit overlooking the ocean from the heights overhanging. She swept her hair from her eyes, from her forehead, and felt the rush of wings about her, the talons fastening into the back of her neck as they seized her and carried her to the church. They held her by the arms and she stood silent waiting as Don Gesualdo unbolted the door. They bore her bodily into the cooler space of the church and she smelt the pungence of incense mixed with brine in the air. The image of the Virgin in her sky-blue mantle flickered behind tiers of candles that stood, sides encrusted with coursing flows of wax, like puddles and rivulets of molten tears and they held her by the back of the neck before the altar, flinging her at the feet of the figure nailed to the cross.

They desired that the wrath of God descend upon her, that the walls run with blood, that the earth be rivven to swallow her, that her tongue be torn out to silence her blasphemy. They wished her eyes be turned to stone, blinded for eternity to unholy visions. They desired it that the suffering Christ refuse her His mercy, that she be turned to a pillar of salt.

But the eyes of the Saviour were lifted above them, raised to the Father, His feet and palms shattered, His sides slashed and battered in His endless passion of redemption, and Maria Pia and His weeping mother knelt beside him, witnessing the fact.

And yet in the tenebrous silence of the chapel a thing began to reveal itself, unfolding in the sunless air. This thing become knowledge that locked itself into hearts now turned aghast—that from that day forward, the housewife would not dare look into the eyes of the shopkeeper, that man and wife would move about each other's presence uneasy, untrusting. They knew that the children standing beside them, eyes downcast, had suddenly seen into places that could not be explained, or even accounted for as were their modest gifts at Epiphany—the magical appearance of sweets and oranges in little shoes placed hopefully by the hearth. The presence of this thing unacknowledged, unspoken, would curl insidiously about the streets and piazzas, stealthily, unimpeded, wisping black under doorways and through cracks in the shutters. They knew, suddenly, that no house was safe from the visitation of the dark angel she had summoned, that it would come like a thief in the night and disturb their sleep, unsettle the chickens in their yards with its passing. And they came to realize that this merciless angel was of their making, not hers. A silence descended on those who accused her, who stood as if they had already taken up the very stones to strike her down, clamouring for murder in the shadow of the cross, amidst the beating of dark wings.

"This is the work of the devil," cried Carlo Treccani, although the eyes of his heart were searching the streets of Napoli for his daughter, whose face he would not find among the dark forms crouching in doorways, a lost face whose cheeks were hollow—perhaps with hunger. It was the voice of his heart that filled the little stone church, like a fall of rain on a garden straining for moisture—a wash of coolness, a silver slick on leaves, blossoms unfolding their scent in the air, grateful. The church filled with the scent of a bower.

The girl beneath the crucifix turned to face them, her arms filled with roses, and the villagers saw her eyes seeking each of them in turn and they felt fall upon them the unfathomable gaze of pity and sorrow of the Mother of All Sorrows.

About the Author

Maryanne Khan was born in Canberra, Australia, and has lived in Milan, Chicago, Brussels, Rome and Washington D.C., before returning to Australia. Her second home is in the North West Frontier Province of Pakistan. Her prose and poetry have been published in anthologies and literary journals in the United States and Australia. Her novel, *Walking to Karachi*, won a 2008 Varuna-HarperCollins Award.

www.ingramcontent.com/pod-product-compliance
Lightning Source LLC
Chambersburg PA
CBHW020729250626
47155CB00006B/2224

* 9 7 8 0 9 8 2 6 0 3 0 4 8 *